PENGUIN 🐧 CLASSICS

VICTORIA

KNUT HAMSUN was born in 1859 to a poor peasant family in central Norway. His early literary ambition was thwarted by having to eke out a living—as a schoolmaster, sheriff's assistant, and road laborer in Norway; as a store clerk, farmhand, and streetcar conductor in the American Midwest, where he lived for two extended periods between 1882 and 1888. Based on his own experiences as a struggling writer, Hamsun's first novel, *Sult* (1890; tr. *Hunger*, 1899), was an immediate critical success. While also a poet and playwright, Hamsun made his mark on European literature as a novelist. Finding the contemporary novel plot-ridden, psychologically unsophisticated, and didactic, he aimed to transform it so as to accommodate contingency and the irrational, the nuances of conscious and subconscious life as well as the vagaries of human behavior. Hamsun's innovative aesthetic is exemplified in his successive novels of the decade: *Mysteries* (1892), *Pan* (1894), and *Victoria* (1898). Perhaps his best known work is *Growth of the Soil* (1917), which earned him the Nobel Prize in 1920. After the Second World War, as a result of his openly expressed Nazi sympathies during the German occupation of Norway, Hamsun forfeited his considerable fortune to the state. He died in poverty in 1952.

SVERRE LYNGSTAD, Distinguished Professor Emeritus of English and Comparative Literature at the New Jersey Institute of Technology, Newark, New Jersey, holds degrees in English from the University of Oslo, the University of Washington, Seattle, and New York University. He is the author of many books and articles in the field of Scandinavian literature, including *Jonas Lie* (1977), *Sigurd Hoel's Fiction* (1984), and *Knut Hamsun, Novelist: A Critical Assessment* (2005). Among his more recent translations from Norwegian are Arne Garborg's *Weary Men* (1999); Sigurd Hoel's *Meeting at the Milestone* (2002); and Knut Hamsun's *Pan* (1998), *On Overgrown Paths* (1999), *Mysteries* (2001), and *The Last Joy* (2003). Dr. Lyngstad is the recipient of several grants, prizes, and awards, and has been honored by the King of Norway with the St. Olav Medal and with the Knight's Cross, First Class, of the Royal Norwegian Order of Merit.

KNUT HAMSUN

Victoria

Translated with an Introduction by
SVERRE LYNGSTAD

PENGUIN BOOKS

PENGUIN BOOKS

Published by the Penguin Group

Penguin Group (USA) Inc., 375 Hudson Street, New York, New York 10014, U.S.A.

Penguin Group (Canada), 90 Eglinton Avenue East, Suite 700, Toronto M4P 2Y3, Canada
(a division of Pearson Penguin Canada Inc.)

Penguin Books Ltd, 80 Strand, London WC2R 0RL, England

Penguin Ireland, 25 St Stephen's Green, Dublin 2, Ireland (a division of Penguin Books Ltd)

Penguin Group (Australia), 250 Camberwell Road, Camberwell, Victoria 3124, Australia
(a division of Pearson Australia Group Pty Ltd)

Penguin Books India Pvt Ltd, 11 Community Centre, Panchsheel Park, New Delhi—110 017, India

Penguin Group (NZ), cnr Airborne and Rosedale Roads, Albany, Auckland 1310, New Zealand
(a division of Pearson New Zealand Ltd)

Penguin Books (South Africa) (Pty) Ltd, 24 Sturdee Avenue, Rosebank, Johannesburg 2196, South Africa

Penguin Books Ltd, Registered Offices:
80 Strand, London WC2R 0RL, England

This translation first published in Penguin Books 2005

3   5   7   9   10   8   6   4   2

Translation, introduction, and notes copyright © Sverre Lyngstad, 2005
All rights reserved

Victoria originally published in Norway in 1898.

LIBRARY OF CONGRESS CATALOGING-IN-PUBLICATION DATA
Hamsun, Knut, 1859–1952.
[Victoria. English]
Victoria / Knut Hamsun ; translated with an introduction by Sverre Lyngstad.
p.   cm.
ISBN 0-14-303937-7
I. Lyngstad, Sverre.   II. Title.
PT8950.H3V4313   2005
839.8'2'36—dc22   2005050950

Printed in the United States of America
Set in Adobe Sabon

For Fiona and Erik
—S.L.

Contents

Introduction

When Hamsun published a fragment of *Hunger*, his break-through novel, in the Danish journal *Ny Jord* (New Earth) in 1888, an event that made him a welcome guest in the drawing rooms of Copenhagen's intellectual luminaries, he had served a literary apprenticeship of more than ten years and experienced life on two continents. His life during those years, as well as afterward, was often one of extreme hardship.

Born to an impoverished peasant family at Skultbakken, Vågå, in central Norway in 1859,[1] Knut Pedersen, to use his baptismal name, had a difficult childhood. In the summer of 1862, when Knut was less than three years old, his father moved with his family to Hamarøy, north of the Arctic Circle, where he worked the farm Hamsund, belonging to his brother-in-law, Hans Olsen. From nine to fourteen Knut was a sort of indentured servant to his uncle, since the family was dependent on him. The boy's beautiful penmanship made him particularly valuable to Hans Olsen, who suffered from palsy and needed a scribe for his multifarious business, from shopkeeper to librarian and postmaster. The uncle treated Knut abominably; he would rap his knuckles with a long ruler at the slightest slip of the pen. And on Sundays the boy had to sit indoors reading edifying literature to Hans and his pietist brethren, painfully aware that his friends were outside, waiting for him to join them. No wonder Knut loved to tend the cattle at the parsonage, where his uncle lived, an occupation that allowed him to lie on his back in the woods dreaming his time away and writing on the sky with his index finger.[2] Very likely, these hours of solitary musings away from the tyranny of his uncle acted as a stimulus to the boy's imagination. His schooling, starting at the age of nine, was sporadic, and his

family had next to no literary culture. However, the local library
at his uncle's place may have provided a modicum of sustenance
for his childish dreams.

During his adolescence and youth Hamsun led a virtually nomadic existence, at first in various parts of Norway, later in the
United States. After being confirmed at Lom, a neighboring
township of Vågå, in 1873, in the same church where he had
been baptized, he was a store clerk in his godfather's business
in Lom for a year, then returned north to work in the same
capacity for a merchant, Mr. Walsøe, not far from his parents'
place. Here, at Tranøy, Knut seems to have fallen in love with
the boss's daughter, Laura. It is uncertain whether the young
man was asked to leave because of his infatuation with Laura,
or because Mr. Walsøe was hurt financially by the failure of the
herring fisheries in 1875.[3] In the next few years Hamsun supported himself as a peddler, shoemaker's apprentice, schoolmaster, and sheriff's assistant in different parts of Nordland.
After the failure of his literary ventures in the late 1870s, the
school of life took the form of road construction work for a
year and a half (1880–81).

Hamsun's dream of becoming a writer had been conceived at
an early age, amid circumstances that gave him no choice but to
fend for himself. If ever a writer can be said to have been self-
made or self-taught, Hamsun was one. Not surprisingly, the two
narratives published in his teens, Den Gådefulde (1877; The
Enigmatic One) and Bjørger (1878), were crude and insignificant, products of literary imitation. The former is an idyllic story
in the manner of magazine fiction, in a language more Danish
than Norwegian. The latter, a short novel, was modeled on the
peasant tales published by Bjørnstjerne Bjørnson (1832–1910)
in the 1850s. In 1879, with the support of a prosperous Nordland businessman, E. B. K. Zahl, Hamsun wrote another novel,
"Frida," which he presented to Frederik Hegel at Gyldendal
Publishers in Copenhagen. It was turned down without comment. The manuscript of this story—which was dismissed by
Bjørnson, Hamsun's idol, as well—has been lost. Bjørnson sug-
gested he become an actor. Thus, in early 1880, shortly after
his twentieth birthday, the first period of Hamsun's literary apprenticeship came to an end.

The 1880s were marked by hard physical labor and renewed literary efforts. During the period he was employed in highway construction, Hamsun made his debut as a public lecturer. His next decision was not unusual for a poor, ambitious Norwegian in the 1880s: emigrating to America. However, he was not chiefly interested in improving his fortune; instead, he foresaw a future for himself as the poetic voice of the Norwegian community in the New World. Needless to say, the dream quickly foundered, though the lecturing activity continued. To support himself he worked as a farmhand and store clerk, except for the last six months or so of his two-and-a-half-years' stay, when he was offered the job of "secretary and assistant minister with a salary of $500 a year" by the head of the Norwegian Unitarian community in Minneapolis, Kristofer Janson (1841–1917).[4] This was Hamsun's first significant encounter with an intellectual milieu. While he did not share Janson's religious beliefs, he clearly enjoyed browsing in his well-stocked library. But his stay was cut short: in the summer of 1884 his doctor diagnosed "galloping consumption," and in the fall of that year Hamsun returned to Norway, apparently resigned to die. He was twenty-five years old. His illness turned out to be a severe case of bronchitis.[5]

Back in Norway, Hamsun's endeavors to support himself by writing stories, articles, and reviews for the newspapers in the capital, Kristiania (now Oslo), while working on a "big book,"[6] brought only a meager harvest financially, despite a considerable amount of publishing activity. Worthy of mention is his article on Mark Twain in the weekly paper *Ny illustreret Tidende* (New Illustrated Gazette) in March 1885, important because by a compositor's error the "d" in his name, Hamsund, was left out.[7] The young aspiring writer adopted this spelling of his name for the rest of his life.

After a couple of years in Norway, at times in severe want, Hamsun returned to America, but now for purely economic reasons: to finance his literary ambition. From New York he wrote a friend in Norway that it had become "impossible" for him at home.[8] However, the challenges posed by America were still formidable. Only toward the end of his two-year stay, after supporting himself as a streetcar conductor in Chicago and a farm laborer in the Dakotas, was he able to turn his attention to literature. Having returned to Minneapolis in the fall of 1887, he delivered a series of lectures there during the winter of 1887–88. These lectures, which dealt with such literary figures as Balzac, Flaubert, Zola, Bjørnson, Ibsen, and Strindberg, attest to Hamsun's painfully acquired familiarity with the literary culture of his time. By July 1888 we find him in Copenhagen. In a brief sketch of his early life recorded in 1894 he says that he "hid on board a day and a half"[9] when the ship reached Kristiania, bypassing the city that had so bitterly frustrated his literary dreams.

The following decade was a very productive period for Hamsun, although his work was not always favorably received. *Hunger* (1890) garnered excellent reviews, but sales were disappointing, and the reception of his second novel, *Mysteries* (1892), was mixed. Moreover, a series of lectures that he gave in the capital and elsewhere in 1891, while causing a sensation, were severely criticized for the high-handed manner in which he dismissed his immediate predecessors on the Norwegian Parnassus. And Hamsun's life, though not exactly nomadic, remained unsettled, as he shuttled back and forth between Kristiania and Copenhagen, between one Norwegian town and another, and—during the period from 1893 to 1895—between Norway and Paris. His restlessness seems to have affected his writing as well, to judge by his forays into different genres. Thus, in the interval between *Pan* (1894) and *Victoria* (1898), Hamsun wrote mainly plays, despite his low opinion of dramatic literature and the theater. In a letter written in August 1898, he says: "I'm tired of the novel, and I've always despised the drama; I've now begun to write verse, the only literature that is not both pretentious and insignificant, but only insignificant."[10] While calling *Victoria* "some sort of 'pendent' [sic] to *Pan*,"[11] he refers to it as "nothing but a little lyricism" and as "full of 'Stimmung.' "[12]

If self-demeaning language were in order, a more appropriate pretext might have been the overall plot of this short fiction, a story of star-crossed lovers separated by class and circumstance. Judged by its plot alone, *Victoria* is pure melodrama. However, as in *Pan,* the plot is merely a framework within which Hamsun creates a web of narrative modes, themes, and motifs, the elements that make up the novel's substance.

Victoria consists of a mosaic of scenes and situations developed according to a basic psychological scheme: dreamlike amorous expectation followed by triumph and, subsequently, by bitter disappointment. Sometimes the second stage is missing, causing the narrative to alternate between hope and disillusion. Yet, the ultimate effect produced by the novel is not one of disillusionment. This may be partly due to a frequently occurring structural pattern in Hamsun's narrative, one whereby a flat rendering of an encounter, mostly couched in clipped, constrained dialogue, is amplified by ecstatic recall and, eventually, literary re-creation. Since Johannes and Victoria see each other so rarely, their meetings usually begin very tentatively and awkwardly, but Johannes' pent-up feelings often break through, as happens in chapter three, where they meet in the city. His ardent confession recapitulates the emotional adventures with which his loving memory of Victoria has enriched him. "I would always see or hear something that reminded me of you, all day, at night too," he tells her. The scene is rounded off by another dialogue sequence, which ends with her telling him, "You're the one I love."

The first part of chapter four employs the same device on a broader scale, as Johannes recalls the entire experience related in chapter three. Being in a state of semidelirious happiness after Victoria's declaration of love, he overwhelms an irate neighbor peeved by his predawn singing with an ecstatic description of his nocturnal experiences. The story he tells him is a heightened version of the previously noted confession to Victoria. He tells the man that, as he was writing during the night, "the heavens were opened, . . . an angel offered me wine and I drank it, intoxicating wine which I drank out of a garnet cup." This possible allusion to the baptism of Jesus also appears in what he related to Victoria the previous day.[13] In both instances, remembrance and literary creation are indistinguishable. For while Johannes tells the neighbor that he "lived it all afresh, one more time," the account he gives him of the meeting with Victoria is a modified version, in some respects quite fanciful. "[W]e met the King," he says, "and the King turned to look at her, at my beloved, because she is so tall and lovely." He goes on to describe what he wrote as "an endless song to joy, to happiness. It was as though happiness lay naked before me with a long, laughing throat and wanted to come to me." That Johannes' happiness is dispelled after he runs into Victoria and Otto, his well-to-do rival, in the theater conforms to the larger rhythm of disenchantment.

This sequence of episode and recollection-*cum*-creative transformation is only one of several strategies whereby Hamsun complicates the narrative flow of the novel. Having the effect of repetition, it produces a sense of recurring cycles of experience, thereby slowing down the pace of the action and mitigating the melodramatic suddenness of key events. The story's climax, Victoria and Otto's engagement party, exhibits another scenic development, equally, if not more, decisive in bracketing the novel's conventional plot. The scene of scandal, which Hamsun had picked up from Dostoyevsky and used successfully in previous works, assumes in *Victoria* an especially outrageous form, since it develops from a celebratory occasion in high society. Again, the opening note, for Johannes, is one of happy anticipation, of which he is cruelly disabused in the course of the party.

In effect, there is a succession of scenes of scandal taking place at the party. Victoria's introduction of Camilla, the girl Johannes had saved from drowning some years earlier, is followed by a series of acrimonious exchanges between Victoria and Johannes reminiscent of the barbed words of Glahn and Edvarda in *Pan*. Johannes is overcome by a "hopeless despair" and turns "deathly pale." Walking around "like an outcast," he gives and receives refined insults, and when he rises to respond to a toast offered him by Richmond, his future rival for the love of Camilla, Johannes suffers a deep humiliation. Taken aback by Victoria's wild outbursts, "her eyes blazing," he is forced to change course and gives a knowingly false retrospective of his relationship with the Castle children. Johannes even implies that his genteel friends had "a large share" in his success as a writer. No wonder Ditlef, Victoria's brother, remarks to his mother, "I never knew it was really me who wrote his books." Obviously upset by the erotic electricity passing between his fiancée and Johannes, Otto, now a lieutenant, warns Victoria by threatening to go hunting with a neighbor, then pokes Johannes in the eye and leaves in a dudgeon.

In view of these occurrences, which contravene ordinary canons of logic and reason, the death of Otto, whether self-inflicted or accidental, becomes quite acceptable. Similarly, the cruel irony of Victoria being turned down when she is finally free to offer herself to Johannes, an irony that under more normal circumstances might seem manufactured, is quite in tune with a state of affairs that has lost all contact with decorum and rational order.

Beyond relating a love story, *Victoria* is a celebration of love in all its facets, its ups and downs, its torments and raptures, its capricious twists and turns. It conjures up the charms of adolescent and youthful love, bright and adventurous or desperately unhappy, as well as the fateful attractions of a besetting passion. While Victoria feels obliged to suppress her love of Johannes and, as a result, becomes a prodigy of dissimulation, with occasional bouts of spite and ill humor, Camilla quickly finds herself in a situation where she simulates a love she does not feel. Here, as in *Pan,* the characters reveal themselves as a cluster of inconsistencies and contradictions. Thus, Victoria will tell Johannes, "You're the one I love," embracing and kissing him while at the same time attempting to palm off Camilla on him. A comic sidelight on the vagaries of Eros is provided by Victoria's former tutor, who, having chosen bachelorhood after the failure of a youthful romance, ends up marrying a widow. The tutor is a perfect foil to the central characters' sublime passions.

The inserted vignettes, or sketches, and the lyrical interludes present a wider array of perspectives on the irrational, and highly ambiguous, workings of desire. The former, mostly depicting situations that involve jealousy and adultery, occasionally assume anomalous forms that, in isolation, would appear implausible or absurd; in context, however, they expand the novel's narrative and psychological horizon. There is, for example, the husband who, having surprised his wife with her lover, asks, "What do you say to putting horns on him—on the one who just left—?" a question that draws a scream from his wife. No less grotesque is the behavior of a loving couple who, as they grow old and decrepit, vie with one another in constancy, to the point that the husband disfigures his face to match his paralyzed wife's "deep furrows" of grief.

By dint of its language, carefully structured by anaphoras and refrain, the main lyrical interlude qualifies as a poem in prose. In this poem, love runs the gamut from being "a yellow phosphorescence in the blood" and a "hot devil's music that set even the hearts of old men dancing" to a "summer night with stars in the sky and fragrance on earth." The imagery ranges from the idyllic ("wind whispering among the roses") to the repellent (a garden of "obscene toadstools"), from nocturnal darkness to flashing suns, from heaven to hell. Ultimately, in a pastiche of Genesis, love becomes "God's first word, the first thought that sailed through his brain. When he said, 'Let there be light!' there was love. . . . And love became the world's beginning and the world's ruler; but all its ways are full of flowers and blood, flowers and blood." Love, or desire, has become an all-encompassing metaphysical principle.

Victoria is unquestionably Hamsun's most erotically charged novel; here, more than anywhere else, love is an inexorable cosmic force; it rules not only the human world but also nature, and Hamsun evokes its omnipresence by a rich array of sensuous images. The "song to joy" of Johannes is duplicated in the forest by the "wild, passionate music" of the birds, the mating call of the blackcock, and the sound of the cuckoo. In her post-engagement confession, Victoria tells Johannes that his voice at the party "was like an organ," and in the postscript to her deathbed letter, Victoria notes that she has "even heard some music." These recurring musical images, together with the images of color—chiefly white, yellow, and red[14]—form a counterpoise to the somewhat ominous connotations of "flowers and blood" in the ambiguous conclusion to the above-cited lyric interlude. They mark a borderland where the experience of Eros coexists with its sublimated forms, such as a felt kinship with all living creatures and the exaltations of artistic inspiration.

With all his attention to Eros as a universal force, Hamsun's emphasis is nevertheless psychological, as he evokes the complexities of individual erotic experience and the ambiguities of artistic creation. The former are most memorably portrayed through Victoria and Camilla. Although the two women form part of a replicating structure, a kind of round with changing partners, they are nicely individualized. Victoria, a near relation of *Pan*'s Edvarda, is torn apart by conflicting emotions; to her, love approaches a perpetual torment, occasionally interrupted by moments of transcendent rapture. Though the color red is associated with both women, it acquires—together with yellow, the color of joy—a deeper resonance in the case of Victoria: her red hat and parasol, unlikely emblems of passion, are eventually replaced by the red of a hemorrhage, the harbinger of a species of love-death. These symbolic touches are, in Victoria's case, supported by nonverbal techniques with a behaviorist slant. In the dialogues of Johannes and Victoria, a language of gesture complements the brief verbal exchanges. Victoria's lips, face, eyes, and hands speak when her tongue is tied. Her lips tremble, she drops her eyes, and her hands make contact, although otherwise she appears cold and unapproachable. But we also hear Victoria's own voice, in a couple of monologues muted by no inhibiting constraints. Edvarda is given no such opportunity in *Pan;* she has to wait until the publication of *Rosa* (1908), a novel in which she appears, before she can give voice to her true feelings. By comparison with Victoria, Camilla is appropriately superficial, a bundle of bad faith but a perfect embodiment of one face of love, inconstancy, and Victoria's diametrical opposite.

Fascinating as these two young women are, the novel's central focus is nevertheless Johannes as a developing writer. Already as a child he cuts "letters and signs" into stones found in the abandoned quarry, one of his favorite haunts. Both the quarry, which he envisages as a cave, and the sea, which also gives rise to romantic fantasies, are images of depths to be explored. His dream of becoming a diver is accidentally fulfilled when, at the age of eighteen, he saves Camilla from drowning. These spaces of refuge and exploration are complemented by images of isolation and power, like being a fearsome "maker of matches" or the ruler of an island guarded by a gunboat. In these images and fantasies creativity is associated with human detachment, an association that the novel will bear out.

Johannes' two passions, for Victoria and literary art, are interestingly interrelated in the book. They can scarcely be separated. All his poetry is written for her, and his "big book," completed after years of emotional frustration but before the official engagement of Victoria and Otto, is a transparent reworking of his youthful experiences transposed into the future. We are given his envisioned conclusion to the book, a meeting at an inn between a no-longer-young, graying man and the lady of the castle, easily recognizable as Victoria by her yellow dress. In the emotional scene that ensues, the man sates his pride in a bitter speech, followed by a prayer for forgiveness. One may note that the scene ends with the lady confessing her love and that the very words she uses, "I love you; do not misunderstand me anymore, you are the one I love. Good-bye!" echo Victoria's declaration of love for Johannes in chapter three. These literary reworkings look like a further development of the pattern demonstrated above, in which the past is creatively transformed. Already in Johannes' recollections, events are modified, telescoped, and viewed at a distance: the borderline between *Wahrheit* and *Dichtung* is a fluid one. Whatever the motive, in his life as in his art, Johannes creates an imagined world: experience is always mediated.

All this creative activity appears to have an underlying *telos*: to counter, if not transcend, time's ineluctable passage and, ultimately, death. Passion-love is one way of suspending mutability, and, like Nagel in *Mysteries,* Johannes stakes the meaning of his entire existence on his love. Unlike Nagel, the artist manqué, however, he finds a credible substitute in his writing when love fails.

As shown in chapter five, Victoria's rejection of him confronts Johannes with existential absurdity. Isolated in the city after Victoria's departure, he finds himself at point zero, prey to macabre fantasies of death and dying. Nature itself is dead: the old poplars outside are "stripped of their leaves and look like miserable freaks of nature; some gnarled branches grinding against the wall produce a creaking sound, like a wooden machine, a cracked stamping mill that runs and runs." In this ambience of decrepitude and decay, Johannes is writing about a "lush, green garden near his home, the Castle garden. . . . It's dead and covered with snow now, and yet that is what he's writing about, and it isn't winter with snow at all, but spring with fragrance and mild breezes." And Victoria, when she appears, does not sport yellow or red but is dressed in white: "She appears like a white spirit in the middle of the green garden."

The reversal of the seasons has a counterpart in Johannes's work habits: he writes at night, when most people are asleep. Paradoxically, the whistle of a train around midnight is a wake-up call: "it sounds like a lone cock crow in the silent night."

The outer limit of Johannes' manipulation of time amounts to downright revolt. Overcome by "violent emotion" after being turned down by Victoria, he gives in to an impulse that can only be described by an oxymoron, "gleeful indignation": tearing a handful of leaves off his calendar, he creates a virtual future moment, which he decides to enjoy to the full smoking his pipe. Unable to locate his pipe cleaner, he "jerks one hand off the corner clock to clean his pipe with." These infractions of temporal order afford him great pleasure. His two-pronged assault on temporality signifies a fundamental aspiration: to create a suspended moment. Just as inspiration or creative activity plays fast and loose with real time, so the literary representation itself aims to concentrate experience in a moment, thus resisting the inroad of destructive time.

In presenting the inner world of Johannes, Hamsun once more shows a preference for indirect methods of portrayal, though different from those used in laying bare the feelings of Victoria. Notable is his use of free indirect discourse, frequently with a strong expressionist slant. Thus, after saying good-bye to Victoria, who warns him not to pursue her, Johannes' state of mind is rendered as follows: "The street stretched cold and gray before him, it looked like a belt of sand, an endless road to walk." The sights he observes in the street, in particular a sickly little boy with "hollow cheeks" and a disfiguring hair disease, are equally imbued with his despondent mood, as is his surmise that the boy's soul was "all withered." The lightening of Johannes' mood is signaled by some ensuing observations, as he imagines the boy watching the other children at play: "Who knows, maybe he sat there being happy about something, maybe he had a doll in his little backstairs room, a jumping jack or a whirligig. Maybe he hadn't lost everything in life, leaving some hope in his withered soul." The point here is not to describe the life of the streets as much as to show, by indirection, the phases of Johannes's consciousness as he struggles to recover from his grievous disappointment. In contrast, his excitement at being invited to Victoria's party comes through perfectly in the following sentence: "The afternoon was calm and warm; the river throbbed like a pulse as it flowed through the steamy landscape."

The technique of free indirect discourse does, however, encompass another horizon beyond that represented by the fictional character, namely, that of the implied narrator. Though the narrator's point of view is nearly identical with that of Johannes, there are passages where the narrator and the central character part company. For example, the writings of Johannes as exemplified by the scene at the inn referred to above are far less complex than the novel in which they appear; that novel also possesses a greater emotional amplitude. Johannes' literary work is motivated by two diametrically opposed passions, amorous devotion and a lover's revenge; the novel transcends these simplicities. In fact, whereas Johannes the writer shapes experience into ready-made patterns, the novel radically undermines such patterns.

The most convincing example showing that the narrator constitutes an independent entity that is larger than the main character's consciousness is Johannes' macabre dream at the end of chapter five, immediately after he has envisioned the conclusion to his "big book." At the same time, the dream offers some fascinating insights into Johannes' subconscious. Now that his double in the nearly finished book has been reassured of his lady's love, Johannes feels triumphant. So what could possibly be wrong? The dream, which ends with a mocking echo of Johannes' childhood wish to become a diver, a motif associated with artistic aspirations, offers some clues.

The context of the dream is one of felt artistic accomplishment on the part of the dreamer: with his book he has won "the kingdom," but the fairy-tale princess has eluded him. From this perspective, the dream evokes the complementary negative state to Johannes' literary triumph. His psyche is at a point of stagnancy; it has nourished his art, symbolized by music, words, and dance, with blood and precious time. No wonder the dreamer is anxious. The encounter with the captive of the mountain alludes to Johannes' childhood threat that he will go into service with a mountain giant to escape the miseries of life and the torment of unrequited love. The dream, however, suggests that this option is a dead end; in any case, the dreamer cannot liberate the giant, who seems to symbolize the state of Johannes' creative self. Instead, it looks as though the dreamer may be in danger of losing his humanity, or his very identity, through the shadow-collecting man of musk. We do not know what lies beyond the bridge that he guards, but the sight of this man instills a "chilling horror" in the dreamer. Though rescue is at hand through the rolling skull, a kind of psychopomp which leads him to the sea and Victoria,[15] the latter, naked and smiling, is unreachable, being defended by a monster, a kind of Nordic Cerberus of the deep that prevents Johannes from enacting his desire. The dream ends in nightmare: when Johannes, the dreamer, calls to Victoria, "he hears his own scream—and wakes up."

The dream seems almost too complex for the context. It certainly undermines, for the reader, Johannes' sense of triumph at the completion of his book. To an outsider, the dream clearly associates artistic endeavor with emotional deadness; it also suggests that an arduous journey of the soul is required to overcome that deadness. However, the scream of terror that concludes the journey of the dreamer betrays Johannes' inability to meet Victoria's challenge. If the monster is viewed as a part of his own psyche, it becomes an emblem of sexual fear. This suspicion is confirmed not only by Johannes's calm indifference when confronted with Camilla's fickleness, but also by his failure to seek out Victoria after Otto's death.

From the perspective of the dream, Johannes' brutal words, "I'm engaged," in response to Victoria's passionate avowal of her love come to seem like a cover for the cooling of his desire. Now that his passion has been exploited for artistic creation and embodied in his work, it is no longer alive: Johannes has attained a condition of emotional stasis. On the one hand, the idea of a poem in which he imagines the earth "seen from above, like a beautiful, fantastic papal gown," with couples walking about in its folds at the "hour of love," makes him feel as though he could "embrace the whole earth"; but, on the other hand, this general love for humanity goes hand in hand with emotional coldness toward individuals. Meeting Camilla and her family in the street, he thinks, "How little it all concerned him, this carriage, these people, this chatter! A cold, empty feeling invaded him. . . ." This coldness may be a reason why Hamsun ended the novel with Victoria's deathbed confession, warm and spontaneous and expressive of an opposing perspective. In her tragic defeat, Victoria paradoxically looks like a winner.

Victoria could be called a Künstlerroman; it is also an example of metafiction, since it problematizes the relationship between lived experience and its artistic representation. That relationship is not a simple one. On the one hand, art is present as an element of everyday life: in our retrospections we reshape the events of our lives in a more expressive and harmonious, though not always truthful, way. Further, much of what is called art often distorts experience, creating compensatory fictional worlds the unstated purpose of which is to magnify our egos. This may lead to spiritual sterility, unless one guards against the emotional indifference—necessary for art but fatal to life—that artistic detachment might produce.

The style of *Victoria* is well suited to its subject. The beginning of the book is written in a fairy-tale manner, describing the world of Johannes as that of a young dreamer who wants to win the princess and half the kingdom. Later, the fairy-tale quality recedes, but not the stylization that the manner of fairy-tale narrative entails. Instead of being described in detail, with circumstantial realism, scenes and situations are rendered sparely, as in legends or myths; thus, places are only vaguely indicated, as is the chronology. Consequently, the book instills a reader attitude that does not ask for the reasons why things occur. *Victoria* creates a fictional world in which rigorous notions of time, space, and cause and effect do not obtain. Its success or failure depends on whether it creates a feeling of empathy in the reader, a sense that, however abstract, it renders life, passion, and artistic creation in a manner that is both true and aesthetically satisfying.

A novel like *Victoria*, whose central characters in their emotional intensity sometimes appear like emblematic figures, like passions and aspirations incarnate, invites critical hyperbole. Its alternation of everyday scenes with high-pitched speeches is suggestive of the recitatives and arias of an operatic performance. Though ordinary enough, in their pride and vehemence the characters are larger than life, driven by impossible desires. As previously mentioned, Eros is expressed by musical motifs, and other images—the cave, the sea, the garden, the creaking poplars—likewise turn up, much like phrases or leitmotifs in a sonata or symphony. Fittingly, the novel concludes with the organ fugue of Victoria's deathbed farewell.

With one exception, which Hamsun deeply resented, the novel was well received by the critics when it appeared in October 1898. Hamsun, who had married an upper-class divorcée, Bergljot Goepfert, in May of the same year, was criticized by Nils Vogt, editor of the conservative *Morgenbladet,* for his "unfamiliarity with" and inability to portray "really fine ladies," and for misrepresenting upper-class Norwegians in general.[16] Subsequent critics have, to my knowledge, found no fault with Hamsun's character portrayal, while more than one have had harsh words for the novel's conventional aspects, using disparaging terms like "innocuous idyll" and "puppet-theatre plot."[17] Edwin Muir, calling *Victoria* one of the "most exquisite" of Hamsun's works, praises the characterization. As a portrayer of women Hamsun belongs, in Muir's view, in the same class as Thomas Hardy. Though they are merely sketched, he writes, Victoria and Camilla "give that sense of a truth existing in them beyond the reach of observation or analysis which, like the creation of the highest imagination in poetry, has a touch of the occult."[18] John Updike, whose review of the Stallybrass translation of *Victoria* is more mixed, sounds a similar note, describing Hamsun as a "heathen visionary" of "intuitive genius" on the strength of the novel.[19]

Not surprisingly, the novel struck a strong emotional chord among critics and readers alike. A Dane who published a book about Hamsun in 1929 said that, for his generation, *Victoria* was what Goethe's *Werther* had been to youth one hundred years earlier.[20] Kurt Wais, the German comparatist, called *Victoria* a work of unprecedented "emotional resonance," and Thomas Mann, who read the novel as a young man, named both *Victoria* and *Pan* "immortal poems."[21] In a more personal vein, Martin Nag reported that, according to the wife of Mikhail Bulgakov, author of *The Master and Margarita,* she and her husband found each other through their "shared love of *Victoria.*"[22]

Such widespread critical acclaim, together with the empathetic response of readers, testifies to the psychological depth of the work. The reputation of the book has not waned: George Steiner, in a recent review of *Hunger,* writes that *Victoria* remains, along with *Pan,* a "powerful, even seductive text," and Robert Ferguson includes the novel as one of Hamsun's "four great novels from the 1890s,"[23] a judgment with which I fully concur. Though the tale of Johannes and Victoria is outwardly simple, it encapsulates a dense and diverse texture, with a rich array of themes and motifs—love's predicament in a class-bound society, erotic passion and artistic creativity, ever-renewed hope followed by disillusionment, zest for life and untoward death. The resulting literary structure, complex and many-voiced, manifests a modernist sensibility and calls for a nuanced response tempering empathy with detachment.

Notes

1. The traditional place of birth has been reported as Garmotrædet, Lom, but Lars Frode Larsen has documented that, although the boy was baptized in Garmo, Lom, where the family had lived, Hamsun had been born in Vågå (*Den unge Hamsun* [Oslo: Schibsted, 1998], 29).

2. Hamsun describes this part of his childhood experience in the travel book *In Wonderland,* trans. Sverre Lyngstad (Brooklyn, N.Y.: Ig Publishing), 107–8.

3. Larsen, *Den unge Hamsun,* 84.

4. Letter to Svend Tveraas of February 29, 1884, in *Knut Hamsuns brev,* ed. Harald S. Næss, I (Oslo: Gyldendal, 1994): 42; Knut Hamsun, *Selected Letters,* ed. Harald Næss and James McFarlane, I (Norwich, England: Norvik Press, 1990): 42. Hereafter referred to as *Brev* and *Letters,* respectively. The translations of letters not in the English edition are my own.

5. Harald Næss, *Knut Hamsun* (Boston: Twayne Publishers, 1984), 12–13.

6. Letter to Nikolai Frøsland of January 19, 1886, *Brev,* I: 53.

7. Hamsun had used the spelling without a "d" in correspondence before the Mark Twain article appeared. See letter to Nikolai Frøsland of January 8, 1885, *Brev,* I: 57 and note 6, same page; *Letters,* I: 52, 254.

8. Letter to Erik Frydenlund of September 4, 1886, *Brev,* I: 69; *Letters,* I: 58.

9. Letter to Bolette and Ole Larsen of November 1894, *Brev,* I: 431; *Letters,* I: 214.

10. Letter to Gerda Welhaven of August 23, 1898, *Brev,* II (Oslo, 1995): 86.

11. Letter (in English) to Albert Langen of September 27, 1898, *Brev,* II: 88.

12. Letters to Georg Brandes of Christmas Eve, 1898, *Brev,* II: 109, and to Albert Langen (in English) of November 20, 1898, *Brev,* II: 92.

13. See Matt. 3:16.

14. An article by Beverly D. Eddy explores the similarities between Hamsun's use of color symbolism in *Victoria* and that of the painter Edvard Munch, whose works of the 1890s as represented by the so-called "Frieze of Life" often strike the viewer as illustrative of Hamsun's obsessive psychological themes. —"Hamsun's *Victoria* and Munch's *Livsfrisen*: Variations on a Theme," *Scandinavian Studies* 48 (1976): 158–60.

15. Atle Kittang views this as an "Orphic fantasy," namely, Johannes' descent into the underworld in search of Victoria. —"Kjærleik, dikting og sosial røyndom: Knut Hamsuns *Victoria*," in *Litteraturhistoriske problem* (Oslo: Universitetsforlaget, 1975), 216.

16. Letters to Georg Brandes of Christmas Eve and November 25, 1898, *Brev,* II: 109 and 96, note 3; *Letters,* II (Norwich, England: Norrik Press, 1998): 21.

17. *Times Literary Supplement,* May 17, 1923, 341; John Updike, "Love as a Standoff," *The New Yorker* 45, June 28, 1969, 93.

18. Edwin Muir, "A Great Writer," *The Freeman* 7, August 8, 1923, 522.

19. Updike, 94–95.

20. Cai M. Woel, *Knut Hamsun* (København, 1929), 6.

21. Kurt Wais, "Knut Hamsuns Wandern durch die Welt," in *An den Grenzen der Nationalliteraturen* (Berlin, 1958), 265; *"Die Weiber am Brunnen"* (*Prager Presse,* January 29, 1922), in Thomas Mann, *Gesammelte Werke in zwölf Bänden* X: *Reden und Aufsätze* (Oldenburg, 1960): 621.

22. Martin Nag, *Hamsun i russisk åndsliv* (Oslo, 1969), 93.

23. George Steiner, in *The Observer Review,* January 26, 1997; Robert Ferguson, *Enigma: The Life of Knut Hamsun* (New York: Farrar, Straus & Giroux, 1987), 177.

Suggestions for Further Reading

Bale, Kjersti. "Hamsuns hvite hest. Om *Victoria.*" *Edda,* 1997: 292–302.

Eddy, Beverly D. "Hamsun's *Victoria* and Munch's *Livsfrisen:* Variations on a Theme." *Scandinavian Studies* 48 (1976): 156–168.

Buttry, Dolores. "Music and the Musician in the Works of Knut Hamsun." *Scandinavian Studies* 53 (1981): 171–82.

Enright, D. J. "Blossoms and Blood: On Knut Hamsun." In *Man Is an Onion.* London: Chatto & Windus, 1972. 52–58.

Evensen, Per Arne. " 'L'orgue saigne' ou le démon de l'ecriture." Trans. Regis Boyer. In *Présence de Hamsun,* ed. Regis Boyer and Jean-Marie Paul. Nancy, France: Presses Universitaires, 1994. 73–94.

Ferguson, Robert. *Enigma: The Life of Knut Hamsun.* New York: Farrar, Straus & Giroux, 1987.

Friese, Wilhelm. "Hamsun und der Jugendstil." *Edda* 67 (1967): 427–49.

Fürstenberg, Hilde. *Die Frauengestalten in Werk und Leben Knut Hamsuns.* Molln in Lauenburg, 1971.

Kittang, Atle. "Kjærleik, dikting og sosial røyndom: Knut Hamsuns *Victoria.*" In *Litteraturhistoriske problem.* Oslo: Universitetsforlaget, 1975. 203–33.

Larsen, Hanna Astrup. *Knut Hamsun.* New York: Knopf, 1922.

McFarlane, James W. "The Whisper of the Blood: A Study of Knut Hamsun's Early Novels," *PMLA* 71 (1956): 563–94.

Næss, Harald. *Knut Hamsun.* Boston: Twayne Publishers, 1984.

Trana, Nils Filip. "Knut Hamsun: *Victoria.* En analyse." Thesis, University of Oslo, 1961.

Updike, John. "Love as a Standoff," *The New Yorker* 45, June 28, 1969, 90, 93–95.

Victoria

I

The miller's son was walking around, thinking. He was a husky fellow of fourteen, tanned with sun and wind and full of all sorts of ideas.

When he grew up he wanted to be a maker of matches. It was so deliciously dangerous; he would get sulphur on his fingers, making everybody afraid to shake hands with him. His comrades would stand in awe of him because of his sinister trade.

He was looking for his birds in the woods. He knew them all, knew where their nests were, understood their cries and answered them with different calls. More than once he had given them pellets of dough made of flour from his father's mill.

All these trees along the path were friends of his. In the spring he had drawn sap from them, and in the winter he had been almost like a father to them, clearing away the snow so the branches would spring back. And even up in the abandoned granite quarry no stone was a stranger to him; he had cut letters and signs in them and raised them up, arranging them like a congregation around a parson. Ever so many wonderful things were going on in this old quarry.

He turned off the path and came down to the pond. The mill was running, a big, booming noise came at him from every side. He was used to wandering about here talking aloud to himself; every bubble of foam had, as it were, a little life of its own to relate, and over by the sluice the water fell straight down, looking like a bright-colored fabric hung out to dry. In the pond below the fall there were fish; he had stood there with his rod many a time.

When he grew up he wanted to be a diver. That was a sure

thing. Then he would go down into the ocean from the deck of a ship and come to strange lands, to kingdoms with swaying forests, vast and mysterious, and with a coral palace on the ocean floor. And the princess waves to him from a window and says, Come in!

Then, from behind, he hears his name being called; his father was shouting "Johannes" to him: "They have sent for you at the Castle. You are to row the young folks over to the island!"

He hurried off. A great, new favor had been granted the miller's son.

In the green landscape, the manor house looked like a small castle—indeed, like a fantastic palace in the solitude. It was a white-painted wooden building with many arched windows in the walls and on the roof, and from its round tower a flag flew whenever the family had visitors. People called it the Castle. Beyond the manor was the bay on one side, and on the other the great forests; in the distance a few small peasant houses could be seen.

Johannes showed up at the quayside and took the young people on board. He knew them from before, they were the Castle children and their city friends. They were all in high boots for wading, except for Victoria, who, wearing only a pair of small dancing shoes and being no more than ten years old anyway, had to be carried ashore when they reached the island.

"Shall I carry you?" Johannes asked.

"May I!" said Otto, a city gentleman of about fifteen, taking her in his arms.

Johannes stood and watched as she was carried ashore, well beyond the water's edge, and he heard her say thank you. Then Otto said over his shoulder, "You'll look after the boat, okay. What's his name anyway?"

"Johannes," Victoria replied. "Sure, he'll look after the boat."

He was left behind. The others headed for the interior of the island, with baskets in their hands for gathering birds' eggs. He stood awhile pondering; he would have loved to go with the others, the boat could simply have been pulled ashore. Too heavy? It was not too heavy. And grabbing hold of the boat, he pulled it up a way.

He could hear the young people laughing and talking as they

started off. All right, 'bye for now. But they could just as well have let him come along. He knew of nests he could have taken them to, curious hidden holes in the cliffs inhabited by birds of prey with bristles on their beaks. Once he had even seen a weasel.

He shoved the boat off and started rowing around to the other side of the island. He had rowed quite a distance when there came a shout: "Row back! You're scaring the birds."

"I just wanted to show you where the weasel is," he replied uncertainly. He waited for a moment. "And how about smoking out the viper's nest? I've brought matches."

There was no answer. He turned the boat and rowed back to the landing place. He pulled the boat ashore.

When he grew up he would buy an island from the Sultan and forbid all access to it. A gunboat would protect its shores. Your Honor, his slaves would report, a ship is riding on the reef, it has run aground, the young people on board will perish. Let them perish! he replies. Your Honor, they're calling for help, we can still save them, and there is a woman in white among them. Save them! he commands in a thundering voice. Then, after many years, he sees the Castle children again, and Victoria throws herself at his feet and thanks him for rescuing her. Never mind, it was only my duty, he replies; go freely wherever you wish in my lands. And he orders the castle gates to be opened for the company and regales them with food from golden plates, and three hundred chocolate-colored slave girls sing and dance all night long. But when the Castle children are to leave, Victoria cannot go through with it; she prostrates herself before him and sobs, because she loves him. Let me stay here, do not turn me away, Your Honor, make me one of your slave girls. . . .

He begins to walk quickly across the island, shivering with excitement. All right, he would rescue the Castle children. Who knows, maybe they had gone astray on the island by now? Maybe Victoria had got stuck between two rocks and couldn't break free? All he had to do was to stretch out his arm and liberate her.

But when he appeared, the children looked at him in amazement. Had he abandoned the boat?

"I hold you responsible for the boat," Otto said.

"Maybe I could show you where the raspberries are?" Johannes said.

Silence among the company. But Victoria jumped at it. "Really? Where would that be?"

But the city gentleman quickly got hold of himself and said, "This is not the time to concern ourselves with that."

"I also know where we can find mussels," Johannes said.

Another silence.

"Are there pearls in them?" Otto asked.

"What if there were!" Victoria said.

Johannes replied that he knew nothing about that, but the mussels were way out, on the white sand. You needed a boat, and you had to dive for them.

Then the idea was thoroughly laughed down, and Otto remarked, "A fine diver you would make!"

Johannes began to breathe hard. "If you like, I can climb that cliff over there and roll a large stone into the sea," he said.

"What for?"

"Oh, for nothing. Well, you could watch me."

But this suggestion wasn't accepted either and, mortified, Johannes fell silent. Then he started looking for eggs far away from the others, in another part of the island.

When the whole party was again gathered down by the boat, Johannes had many more eggs than the others; he carried them carefully in his cap.

"How come you found so many?" the city gentleman asked.

"I know where the nests are," Johannes replied happily. "I'm putting them together with yours, Victoria."

"Stop!" Otto yelled. "Why?"

Everyone looked at him. Otto pointed at the cap and asked, "Who can assure me that that cap is clean?"

Johannes didn't say a word. His happiness was suddenly gone. He began to wend his way back across the island with the eggs.

"What's the matter with him? Where is he going?" Otto says impatiently.

"Where are you going, Johannes?" Victoria calls and runs after him.

Stopping, he answers quietly, "I'm putting the eggs back in the nests."

They stood awhile looking at each other.

"And this afternoon I'm going up to the quarry," he said.

She didn't answer.

"I could show you the cave."

"But I'm so scared," she replied. "You said it was so dark."

Then Johannes smiled, for all his sadness, and said bravely, "Yes, but I'll be with you, you know."

He had always played in the old granite quarry.

People had heard him talk as he worked up there, although he was alone; sometimes he had been a parson and held a service.

The place had long since been abandoned; moss was growing on the rocks, and almost all traces left by drills and wedges had been erased. But the miller's son had cleared the interior of the secret cave and decorated it with great artfulness, and there he lived as chieftain of the world's most daring robber band.

He rings a silver bell. A little manikin, a dwarf with a diamond clip in his cap, hops in. This is his valet. He prostrates himself before him. When Princess Victoria comes you will show her in! Johannes says in a loud voice. The dwarf prostrates himself once more and disappears. Johannes stretches himself easefully on the soft divan and ponders. That's where she would be seated, while he offered her elegant dishes from receptacles of gold and silver; the cave would be illuminated by a blazing fire, and deep inside, behind a heavy curtain of gold brocade, her bed would be made, guarded by twelve knights. . . .

Johannes gets up, crawls out of the cave and listens. There is a rustle among the twigs and leaves on the path. "Victoria!" he calls.

"Yes," comes the reply.

He goes to meet her. "I don't think I dare," she says.

Rocking his shoulders, he answers, "I've just been there. I came back this minute."

They enter the cave. He motions her to sit down on a stone and says, "That's the stone the giant sat on."

"Ooh, not another word, don't tell me! Weren't you scared?"

"No."

"You said he had only one eye, but it's the trolls who have that."

Johannes thought it over. "He had two eyes, but he was blind in one of them. He told me so himself."

"What more did he say? No, don't tell me!"

"He asked me if I would enter his service."

"Oh, but surely you wouldn't? God forbid!"

"Well, I didn't say no. Not definitely."

"Are you mad! Do you want to be locked up inside the mountain?"

"Well, I don't know. It's miserable here on earth too."

Pause.

"After those city boys came, you've been with them all the time," he says.

Another pause.

"Still, you know, I'm stronger than any of them for carrying you and for lifting you out of the boat," Johannes continues. "I'm sure I could stand holding you for a whole hour. Look!"

He took her in his arms and lifted her. She held on to his neck.

"All right, but now you don't have to stand me anymore."

He put her down. "But Otto is also strong," she said. "He has even fought with grownups."

"With grownups?" Johannes asks doubtfully.

"Yes, he has. In town."

Pause.

Johannes ponders. "Well," he says, "that's that. I know what I'll do."

"What will you do?"

"I'll go into service with the giant."

"Oh no! Say, are you mad?" Victoria screams.

"Oh, yes, that's what I'll do. I don't care."

Victoria thinks of a way out. "But perhaps he won't be back anymore now."

"He'll be back," Johannes replies.

"Here?" she asks quickly.

"Yes."

Victoria gets up and withdraws to the mouth of the cave. "Come, we'd better leave."

"No need to hurry," says Johannes, who has himself turned pale. "He won't be here until tonight. On the stroke of midnight."

Victoria calms down and is about to go back to her seat. But

Johannes finds it difficult to overcome the uneasiness he has himself awakened and, feeling the cave has become too dangerous for him, he says, "If you insist on leaving, I do have a stone with your name on it out there. I'll be glad to show it to you."

They crawl out of the cave and find the stone. Victoria is proud and happy. Johannes is touched and says, almost in tears, "You must think of me now and then when you look at it while I'm away. Send me a friendly thought."

"Certainly," Victoria answers. "But you'll come back, won't you?"

"Oh, God knows. No, I probably won't."

They started walking homeward. Johannes is close to tears.

"Good-bye, then," Victoria says.

"No, I can walk you a little farther."

However, her callous readiness to say good-bye to him—the sooner the better—makes him feel bitter and kindles anger in his lacerated heart. Stopping abruptly, he says with righteous indignation, "But I can tell you one thing, Victoria: you will never find anybody who would be as kind to you as I. I can tell you that much."

"But Otto is also kind," she retorts.

"All right, take him."

They walk a few steps in silence.

"I'll do just fine, don't you worry. You don't know yet how much I'll get in wages."

"No. What will you get?"

"Half the kingdom. For one."

"Fancy that! You will, really?"

"And I'll have the princess too."

Victoria stops. "That's not true, is it?"

"Oh yes, that's what he said."

Pause. Victoria mutters to herself, "I wonder what she looks like."

"Oh, good Lord, she's more beautiful than any earthly woman. Well, that we knew already."

Victoria is crushed. "So you want her, then?" she asks.

"Yes, I guess it will come to that," he answers. However, seeing that Victoria is really upset, he adds, "But it's quite possible I'll be back some day. That I'll take a trip back to earth again."

"But then you mustn't take her with you," she pleads. "What would you want her with you for?"

"Well, I can come alone."

"Will you promise me that?"

"All right, I promise. But what do you care anyway! I really can't expect you to care about that."

"Don't say such things, I tell you," Victoria answers. "I'm positive she doesn't love you as much as I do."

His youthful heart trembles with a warm delight. He could have sunk into the ground with joy and bashfulness at her words. Not daring to face her, he looks away. Then he picks up a twig from the ground, gnaws off its bark and smacks his hand with it. Finally, in his embarrassment, he begins to whistle.

"Well, maybe I'd better get home," he says.

"Good-bye then," she answers, giving him her hand.

II

The miller's son went away. He was away for a long time, going to school and learning many things; he grew, became big and strong, and began to have down on his upper lip. The town was so far away, the travel to and fro so expensive, that the frugal miller kept his son in town summer and winter for many years. He was studying the whole time.

But now he had turned into a grown man; he was some eighteen or twenty years old.

And so, one spring afternoon, he stepped ashore from the steamer. At the Castle, the flag had been run up for the son, who came home on vacation by the same ship; a carriage had been sent to the pier to pick him up. Johannes tipped his cap to the lord of the manor, his wife, and Victoria. How big and tall Victoria had grown! She didn't return his greeting.

He tipped his cap once again, and he heard her ask her brother, "Tell me, Ditlef, who greeted me just now?"

"That was Johannes, the miller's son," her brother replied.

She gave him another glance or two, but now he was too embarrassed to bow to her again. The carriage drove off.

Johannes went home.

Goodness, how quaint and small the house was! He couldn't

walk upright through the door. His parents received him with a drink. He was seized by an intense emotion, everything was so dear and touching, his father and mother so good and gray as they received him; they held out their hands to him in turn, welcoming him home.

Already the same evening he took a walk to inspect everything: he visited the mill, the quarry and the fishing hole, listened wistfully to the familiar birds, which were already building their nests in the trees, and took a turn over to the enormous anthill in the woods. The ants were gone, the mound deserted. He poked in it, but there was no sign of life anymore. As he wandered about, he noticed that the manorial woods had been badly thinned out.

"Do you still recognize things around here?" his father asked in jest. "Did you meet those old thrushes of yours?"

"I don't recognize everything. The forest has been cut."

"The forest belongs to the Castle," his father said. "It's not for us to count the master's trees. Everyone needs money, the master needs a lot of money."

The days came and went, sweet, mild days, wonderful days in solitude, with tender recollections of childhood, a summons back to the earth and the sky, to the air and the mountains.

He was walking along the road to the Castle. In the morning he had been stung by a wasp and his upper lip was swollen; if he met someone he would simply bow and walk straight on. He met nobody. In the Castle garden he saw a lady, and when he got closer he made a deep bow and strolled past. It was the mistress herself. He still experienced palpitations as in the old days when he walked by the Castle. Respect for the great house and the many windows, for the stern, aristocratic figure of the proprietor, was still in his blood.

He took the road leading to the pier.

Suddenly he ran across Ditlef and Victoria. Johannes felt ill at ease—they were liable to think he was stalking them. Besides, his lip was swollen. He slowed down, uncertain whether to go on. He did. While still far off he bowed and removed his cap, holding it in his hand as he passed. They both answered his greeting in silence and strode slowly by. Victoria looked straight at him; her face changed slightly.

Johannes continued down to the jetty; he had been seized by

restlessness and his walk became nervous. How tall Victoria had become, completely grown up, and lovelier than ever! Her eyebrows nearly came together above her nose, they were like two delicate lines of velvet. Her eyes had turned darker, a very dark blue.

When on his way home, he turned into a path that led through the forest well beyond the Castle garden. Nobody was going to say he was dogging the footsteps of the Castle children. He reached the top of a hill, picked up a stone and sat down. The birds were making a wild, passionate music, giving their mating calls, pairing off, and flying about with twigs in their beaks. A sweetish smell of earth, of sprouting leaves and rotting trees, hung in the air.

He had happened onto Victoria's path, she was coming straight at him from the opposite direction.

A feeling of helpless irritation came over him, he wished he were far, far away; this time she was bound to think he had been following her. Should he greet her again? Perhaps he could simply look the other way, what with that wasp sting and all.

But when she got close enough, he stood up and tipped his cap. She smiled and nodded. "Good evening. Welcome home," she said.

Again her lips seemed to tremble slightly, but she quickly regained her composure.

"This may appear a bit strange," he said, "but I didn't know you were here, Victoria."

"No, you didn't," she replied. "It was a whim of mine, it just occurred to me to come this way."

Ouch! He had spoken as though he were on intimate terms with her.

"How long will you be home?" she asked.

"Till vacation is over."

He had trouble answering her, she had suddenly become so distant. Why had she spoken to him anyway?

"Ditlef tells me you are such a good student, Johannes. You're doing so well in your exams. And he also tells me you write poetry. Is that true?"

Squirming, he answered curtly, "To be sure. Everyone does."

She would probably soon be on her way, for she said nothing in return.

"Can you believe it, I was stung by a wasp today," he said, showing her his lip. "That's why I look like this."

"Then you have been away for too long, our wasps don't recognize you anymore."

She didn't care whether he had been disfigured by a wasp or not. Very well. She stood there twirling a red parasol on her shoulder, its handle topped with a gold knob, and nothing else concerned her. And yet he had carried the young lady in his arms more than once.

"I don't recognize the wasps," he replied. "They used to be my friends."

But she didn't grasp his deep meaning; she didn't answer. It was such a deep meaning, though.

"I don't recognize anything around here. Even the woods have been cut down."

A light spasm passed across her face.

"Then you probably can't write poetry here?" she said. "What if you wrote a poem to me sometime! Oh, what am I saying! That shows you how little I know about it."

He lowered his eyes, mute and angered. She was making amiable fun of him, speaking snootily and observing what effect it had on him. Begging her pardon, he had not only wasted his time writing, he had also read more than most people. . . .

"Well, I trust we'll meet again. So long."

He doffed his cap and left without answering.

If she only knew that it was to her and no one else he had written his poems, every one of them, even the one to Night, even the one to the Spirit of the Bog. She would never know.

On Sunday Ditlef came and wanted Johannes to go to the island with him. I'm to be the oarsman again, he thought. He went along. Down by the pier some people were taking their Sunday stroll, otherwise everything was very quiet and the sun shone warmly in the sky. Suddenly the sound of music was heard in the distance, it was coming from the sea, from the islands out there; the packet boat was turning in a wide arc as it approached the dock, and it had a band on board.

Johannes untied the boat and sat down at the oars. He was in a soft, lightsome mood this sunny day, and the music from the ship was weaving a veil of flowers and golden grain before his eyes.

Why didn't Ditlef come? He stood on shore watching the people and the ship, as if he weren't going any farther. I won't sit here at the oars any longer, Johannes thought, I'll go ashore. He began turning the boat.

Then he suddenly saw a glimpse of something white and heard a splash in the water; a chorus of desperate, screaming voices rose from the ship and from people on shore, and numerous hands and eyes indicated the spot where the white thing had disappeared. The music was stopped immediately.

Johannes was there in an instant. He acted entirely by instinct, without thinking, without conscious decision. He never heard the mother up on deck screaming, "My little girl, my little girl!" and he no longer saw a single person. He simply jumped from the boat right off and dived in.

For a moment he was gone, for a minute; they could see the water swirling where he had jumped in, and they understood he was working away. On board the ship the wailing continued.

Then he popped up again a bit farther out, several fathoms from the scene of the accident. People shouted to him, gesturing wildly: "No, it was here, it was here!"

And again he dived.

Another agonizing moment, a ceaseless wailing and wringing of hands from a woman and a man on deck. Another man, the mate, jumped out from the ship, having removed his jacket and shoes. He carefully searched the place where the girl had gone down, and everybody pinned their hopes on him.

Then Johannes' head reappeared above the surface, still farther out, several more fathoms. He had lost his cap, his head glistened like the head of a seal in the sun. He was evidently struggling with something, was having difficulty swimming, one hand being tied up. A moment later he had managed to heave something into his mouth, between his teeth, a big bundle; it was the child. Astonished cries reached him from the ship and the shore; even the mate must have heard the new shouts, he shot up his head and looked about him.

Finally Johannes reached his boat, which had drifted off; he got the girl on board and then himself. It was all done without hesitation. People saw him bending over the girl and literally tearing her clothes open in the back; then he seized the oars and rowed up to the ship for all he was worth. The moment the child was snatched up and pulled aboard, a succession of triumphant cheers rang out.

"How come it occurred to you to search so far out?" they asked him.

"I know the ground," he replied. "And then there is a current. I knew that."

A gentleman pushes his way to the ship's side, he is deathly pale; he smiles a twisted smile and there are tears on his eyelashes.

"Come on board for a moment!" he calls down. "I want to thank you. We owe you such a debt of gratitude. Just for a moment."

And the man rushes back from the rail again, deathly pale.

The ports are opened and Johannes steps on board.

He didn't remain there for long; he gave his name and address, a woman embraced the soaking wet young man, and the pale, distraught gentleman slipped his watch into his hand. Johannes entered a cabin where two men were working on the half-drowned girl. "She'll pull through, her pulse is beating!" they said. Johannes looked at the patient, a young blond thing in a short dress; the dress was completely torn in the back. Then a man planted a hat on his head and he was led out.

He had no clear idea how he had got ashore and pulled up the boat. He heard another round of cheers and festive music as the ship steamed away. A wave of rapture, cool and sweet, flowed through him from top to toe; he smiled and his lips moved.

"So there won't be any outing today?" Ditlef said. He looked disgruntled.

Victoria had appeared; she stepped up and said quickly, "Certainly not. Are you crazy! He must get home and change his clothes."

Ah, what a thing to have happened to him, in his nineteenth year at that!

Johannes took to his heels and ran home. The music and the loud hurrahs were still ringing in his ears, he continued being propelled by a powerful excitement. He passed his home and followed the path through the woods up to the granite quarry. Here he looked for a nice, sun-baked spot. His clothes were steaming. He sat down. A wild, joyous restlessness made him get up again and walk about. He was filled to the brim with happiness! Falling on his knees, he thanked God for this day with hot tears in his eyes. *She* had been down there, she'd heard the cheers. Go home and put on dry clothes, she'd said.

He sat down, laughing over and over again in a transport of joy. Yes, she had seen him perform this labor, this heroic deed, she had followed him with pride as he brought in the half-drowned girl by his teeth. Victoria, Victoria! If she just knew how completely, beyond words, he was hers every minute of his life! He would be her servant and slave, sweeping a path before her with his shoulders. And he would kiss her tiny shoes and pull her carriage and lay the fire for her on cold days. He would lay her fire with gilded wood. Ah, Victoria!

He looked about him. Nobody had heard, he was alone with himself. He was holding the precious watch in his hand; it ticked, it was running.

Thanks, oh, thanks for this great day! He patted the moss on the rocks and the fallen twigs. Victoria hadn't smiled at him; oh well, that was not her way. She simply stood there on the pier, a tinge of red fluttering across her cheeks. Maybe she would have accepted his watch if he had given it to her?

The sun was sinking and the heat tapering off. He felt that he was wet. Then he ran homeward, light as a feather.

There were summer visitors at the Castle—a party from the city—and dancing and festive sounds. The flag was flying from the round tower night and day for a week.

There was hay to be brought in, but the horses were kept busy by the merry visitors and the hay remained out. And there were great stretches of unmown meadow, but the hired men were being used as drivers and oarsmen, and the hay remained uncut and dried up.

And the music went on playing in the Yellow Room. . . .

During these days the old miller stopped the mill and locked up his house. He had become so wise; formerly it had happened that the fun-loving city people had come in a body and played pranks with his grain sacks. For the nights were so warm and light and their whims so numerous. The wealthy chamberlain had once, in his younger days, carried a trough with an anthill in it into the mill with his own two hands and left it there. The chamberlain was now a man of mature years, but Otto, his son, who was still coming to the Castle, amused himself in curious ways. Many stories were told about him. . . .

Sounds of hoofbeats and shouting rang through the forest. Some young people were out riding, and the Castle horses were glossy and wild. The horsemen came up to the miller's house, knocked on the door with their whips and wanted to ride in. The door was so low and yet they wanted to ride in.

"Howdy, howdy!" they cried. "We've come to say hello."

The miller laughed humbly at this whim.

Then they dismounted, tied up their horses, and set the mill running.

"The hopper is empty!" screamed the miller. "You'll destroy the mill."

But his words were lost in the crashing noise.

"Johannes!" the miller called at the top of his voice, looking up at the quarry.

Johannes came.

"They're grinding up the mill," his father cried, pointing.

Johannes walked slowly toward the party. He was terribly pale, and the veins in his temples stood out. He recognized Otto, the chamberlain's son, who was wearing a midshipman's uniform; in addition to him there were two others. One of them smiled and bowed, to smooth things over.

Johannes didn't shout, gave no hint, but went straight on. He makes a beeline for Otto. Just then he sees two horsewomen riding up from the woods; one of them is Victoria. She is wearing a green riding habit, and her horse is the white Castle mare. She does not dismount but sits there observing everybody with quizzical eyes.

Then Johannes alters his course. Turning aside, he climbs up on the dam and opens the sluice gate. The noise gradually diminishes, the mill stops.

"No, let it run!" Otto cried. "What are you doing that for? Let the mill run, I tell you."

"Was it you who started the mill?" Victoria asked.

"Yes," he replied, laughing. "Why did it stop? Why can't it run?"

"Because it's empty," Johannes answered breathlessly, look-ing at him. "Do you understand? The mill is empty."

"It was empty, can't you hear?" Victoria said too.

"How was I to know?" Otto said and laughed. "Why was it empty? I ask. Was there no grain in it?"

"Get back on your horse!" one of his comrades cut in, to put an end to it.

They got into their saddles. One of them apologized to Jo-hannes before riding off.

Victoria was the last to leave. After starting to ride away, she turned her horse and came back. "Please ask your father to ex-cuse this," she said.

"It would make more sense if the cadet himself did so," Jo-hannes replied.

"Well, naturally, but still. He's so full of ideas. . . . How long it is since we saw each other, Johannes!"

He looked up at her, wondering if he had heard correctly. Had she forgotten last Sunday, his great day!

"I saw you Sunday on the pier," he replied.

"Oh yes," she said quickly. "How lucky that you were able to help the mate with the search. You did find the girl, the two of you, right?"

Hurt, he replied shortly, "Yes, we found the girl."

"Or was it," she went on, as if something had occurred to her, "was it you alone . . . ? What's the difference anyway. Well, I do hope you will put in a good word with your father. Good night."

Nodding her head and smiling, she gathered up the reins and rode off.

When Victoria was out of sight, Johannes wandered after her into the forest, restless and angry. He found Victoria stand-ing by a tree, quite alone. She was leaning against the tree and sobbing.

Had she been thrown? Had she hurt herself?

He walked up to her and asked, "Have you had an accident?"

She took a step toward him, spread her arms and gave him a radiant look. Then she paused, let her arms fall and replied, "No, I haven't had an accident. I dismounted and let the mare go on ahead. . . . Johannes, you mustn't look at me like that. You were standing at the pond looking at me. What do you want?"

"What I want? I don't understand . . . ," he stammered.

"You are so broad there," she said, suddenly putting her hand on his. "You are so broad there, at your wrist. And you are completely brown from the sun, nut-brown. . . ."

He made a move, wanting to take her hand. But she gathered up her dress and said, "No, nothing happened to me. I just felt like going home on foot. Good night."

III

Johannes went back to the city. And years went by, a long, eventful time of work and dreams, lessons and versifying. He had got a good start, having succeeded in writing a poem about Esther, 'the Jewish girl who became queen of Persia,' a work that appeared in print and earned him some money. Another poem, "The Labyrinth of Love," put into the mouth of Munken Vendt, gave him a name.

What was love? A wind whispering among the roses, no, a yellow phosphorescence in the blood. Love was a hot devil's music that set even the hearts of old men dancing. It was like the marguerite, which opens wide as night comes on, and it was like the anemone, which closes at a breath and dies at a touch. Such was love.

It could ruin a man, raise him up again, and then brand him anew; it could fancy me today, you tomorrow, and someone else tomorrow night, that's how fickle it was. But it could also hold fast like an unbreakable seal and blaze with unquenchable passion until the hour of death, because it was eternal. So, what was the nature of love?

Ah, love is a summer night with stars in the sky and fragrance on earth. But why does it make young men follow secret ways, and old men stand on tiptoe in their lonely rooms? Alas, love turns the human heart into a mildewed garden, a lush and shameless garden in which grow mysterious, obscene toadstools.

Doesn't it make monks prowl by night through closed gardens and press their eyes to the windows of sleepers? And doesn't it possess nuns with foolishness and darken the understanding of princesses? It can knock a king's head in the dust, making his hair sweep the road as he whispers lewd words to himself, laughing and sticking out his tongue.

Such was the nature of love.

No, no, again it was very different, it was like nothing else in the whole world. It came to earth on a spring night when a young man saw two eyes, two eyes. He stared and saw. He kissed two lips—it was as though two flames met in his heart, a sun flashing at a star. He fell into a pair of arms, and he heard and saw no more in the whole wide world.

Love is God's first word, the first thought that sailed through his brain. When he said, "Let there be light!" there was love. And everything that he made was very good, and no part thereof did he wish undone. And love became the world's beginning and the world's ruler; but all its ways are full of flowers and blood, flowers and blood.

A day in September.

This out-of-the-way street was his favorite promenade; here he strolled as in his own room, because he never met anybody, and there were gardens behind both sidewalks, with trees having red and yellow leaves.

How come Victoria is walking here? What can have brought her this way? He was not mistaken, it was she; and perhaps it was she who had walked there also yesterday evening, when he looked out of his window.

His heart was thumping. He knew that Victoria was in town, that he had heard; but she moved in circles the miller's son never entered. Nor did he associate with Ditlef.

He pulled himself together and walked toward the lady. Didn't she recognize him? She just walked on, serious and thoughtful, her head carried proudly on her long neck.

He greeted her.

"Good morning," she answered quite softly.

She didn't make as if to stop and he walked by in silence. His legs twitched. At the end of the little street he turned around, as he was in the habit of doing. I'll keep my eyes glued to the sidewalk and not look up, he thought. Only after a dozen steps or so did he look up.

She had stopped by a window.

Should he slip away, into the next street? What was she standing there for? The window was a poor one, a small store window in which could be seen a few crossed bars of red soap, grits in a glass jar, and some used postage stamps for sale.

Maybe he could continue another dozen steps and then turn back?

At that moment she looked at him, and suddenly she came toward him again. She walked fast, as though she had taken heart, and when she spoke she had difficulty catching her breath. She smiled nervously.

"Good morning. How nice to meet you."

God, how his heart was struggling; it wasn't beating, it trembled. He tried to say something but wasn't able to, only his lips moved. Her clothes gave off a scent, her yellow dress, or perhaps it was her mouth. At that moment he had no clear impression of her face, but he recognized her fine shoulders and saw her long, slender hand on the handle of her parasol. It was her right hand. She was wearing a ring on it.

In the first few seconds he didn't think about this and had no feeling of distress. Her hand was strangely beautiful.

"I've been in town for a whole week," she went on, "but I haven't seen you. Well, yes, I did see you once in the street; somebody told me it was you. You've grown so tall."

"I knew you were in town," he mumbled. "Will you be staying long?"

"A few days. No, not long. I must go home again."

"Thanks for giving me a chance to say hello to you," he said. Pause.

"By the way, I think I've lost my way," she resumed. "I'm staying at the chamberlain's, which way is that?"

"I'll take you there, if I may."

They started walking.

"Is Otto at home?" he asked by way of saying something.

"Yes, he's home," she replied shortly.

Some men came out of a gate carrying a piano between them, blocking the sidewalk. Victoria swerved to the left, bringing her entire body into contact with her companion. Johannes looked at her.

"Pardon me," she said.

A wave of delight flowed through him at this touch, he felt her breath directly on his cheek for a moment.

"I see you're wearing a ring," he said. He smiled, assuming an indifferent air. "May I congratulate you?"

What would she answer? He didn't look at her, holding his breath.

"And you?" she replied, "haven't you got a ring? Oh, you haven't. Actually, someone did tell me . . . One hears so much about you these days, it's all in the papers."

"I've written a few poems," he said. "But I don't suppose you have seen them."

"Wasn't there a whole book? I seem to—"

"Oh yes, there was also a little book."

They came to a square. Though expected at the chamberlain's, she was in no hurry and sat down on a bench. He stood in front of her.

Suddenly she held out her hand to him and said, "You sit down too."

Only after he had sat down did she let go of his hand.

Now or never! he thought. He tried once more to affect a light-hearted, nonchalant tone, smiling and looking at nothing in particular. Good.

"So you're engaged and won't even tell me, is that it? With me being your neighbor back home and all."

She thought it over. "That isn't exactly what I wanted to talk to you about today," she replied.

Turning serious all of a sudden, he said in a low voice, "Oh well, I think I understand anyway."

Pause.

"I knew all along, of course," he resumed, "that it was hopeless for me . . . well, that I wouldn't be the one who . . . I was simply the miller's son, and you . . . Obviously, that's the way it is. I don't even understand how I dare sit here beside you right now and hint at such a thing. Because I ought to stand up before you, or I should be lying over there, on my knees. That would be the correct thing. But I feel as though . . . And all these years I've been away have also left their mark. I seem to be bolder now. After all, I know I'm not a child anymore, and I also know that you can't throw me in prison, even if you wanted to. That's why I dare say this. But you mustn't be angry with me for it, or I'd rather keep silent."

"No, speak out. Say whatever you like."

"May I? Whatever I like? But then your ring couldn't forbid me anything either."

"No," she said softly, "it forbids you nothing. No."

"What? But how am I to take it, then? Well, God bless you, Victoria, unless I'm mistaken?" He jumped up and leaned forward to take a good look at her face. "I mean, doesn't the ring mean anything?"

"Sit down again."

He sat down.

"Oh, you should know how I've been thinking of you; good heavens, has there ever been a thought of someone else in my heart! Of all the people I've seen or known about, you were the only person in the world for me. I couldn't think in any other way: Victoria is the most beautiful and the most magnificent of all, and I know her! *Lady* Victoria, I always thought. Not that I wasn't perfectly aware that nobody could be further away from you than I was, but I knew of you—which was anything but a small thing for me—and that you lived in a certain place and perhaps remembered me once in a while. You didn't, of course; but many an evening I've sat on my chair thinking that perhaps you remembered me once in a while. And then, let me tell you, Lady Victoria, it was as though the heavens were opened to me, and I wrote poems to you and spent what money I had on flowers for you, to take home and put in a glass. All my poems are for you; only a few are not, and they aren't published. But I don't suppose you have read those that are published either. Now I've started on a big book. God, how grateful I am to you! I'm so full of you, and that's all my joy. I would always see or hear something that reminded me of you, all day, at night too. I've written your name on the ceiling, I lie there looking up at it; but the maid who tidies my room can't see it, I've written it very small so I can have it all to myself. It gives me a certain happiness."

She turned away, opened her bodice and took out a piece of paper.

"Look here!" she said, breathing heavily. "I cut it out and kept it. I don't mind telling you, I read it at night. It was Papa who first showed it to me, and I went over to the window to read it. 'Where is it? I can't find it,' I said, turning the page of the newspaper. But I found it easily and was already reading it. And I was so happy."

The paper gave off a fragrance from her breast; she opened it herself and showed it to him, one of his early poems, four brief stanzas to her, to the lady on the white horse. It was a heart's naïve, fervent confession, eruptions that couldn't be held back but leaped up from the lines, like stars coming out in the sky.

"Yes," he said, "I wrote that. It was a long time ago, I wrote it one night when the poplars kept rustling outside my window. Why, you're really going to keep it? Thank you! You've put it away. Ah," he exclaimed, thrilled, speaking in an undertone, "just think how close you are to me right now, sitting here. I can feel your arm against mine, your body radiates warmth. Many a time when I was alone, I shivered with emotion thinking about you; but now I feel warm. The last time I was home you were lovely too, but you're lovelier now. It's your eyes and your eyebrows, your smile—oh, I don't know, it's all of it, everything about you."

She smiled and looked at him with half-closed eyes shining deep blue under her long lashes. Her complexion had a warm glow to it. She seemed overcome by a feeling of intense joy, reaching out to him with an unconscious movement of her hand.

"Thank you!" she said.

"No, Victoria, don't thank me," he replied. Borne toward her heart and soul, as on a tide, he wanted to say more, more; there were confused outbursts, as though he were drunk. "But Victoria, if you love me a little . . . I don't know one way or the other, but tell me you do even if it isn't true. Please! Oh, I would promise you to make something of myself, something great, something almost unheard of. You have no idea what I could make of myself; sometimes when I think hard about it, I feel I'm brimful of things waiting to be done. Many a time my cup is filled to overflowing, and I dance about my room at night because I'm full of visions. There is a man in the next room, he can't sleep and knocks on the wall. At daybreak he comes to my room, furious. That's all right, I don't mind him. By then I've thought about you for so long that you seem to be there with me. I go up to the window and start singing; there is a hint of daylight already and the poplars are rustling outside. 'Good night!' I say, face to face with the morning. That's for you. She's still sleeping, I think to myself. Good night, God bless her! Then I turn in. And so it goes, night after night. But I never imagined you were as lovely as you are. This is how I'll remember you when you're gone, the way you are now. I'll remember you so clearly. . . ."

"You won't be coming home?"

"No. I'm not ready yet. Yes, I'll come. I'm going away now. I'm not ready, I want to do all sorts of things. Do you still wander about in the garden at home sometimes? Do you ever go out in the evening? I could meet you, say hello to you perhaps, that's all. But if you love me a little, if you can bear me, put up with me, then say . . . give me the pleasure . . . Do you know, there is a palm tree that flowers only once in its lifetime, and yet it lives till seventy, the talipot palm. But it flowers only once. I'm flowering now. Sure, I'll get some money and come home. I'll sell what I've written; you see, I'm working on a big book and now I'll sell it, first thing in the morning, all that is finished. I'll get quite a bit for it. So you would like me to come home, eh?"

"Yes."

"Thank you, thank you! Forgive me if I hope for too much, for being too trusting; it's so sweet to be overly trusting. This is the happiest day of my life. . . ."

He took off his hat and placed it beside him.

Victoria looked about her; a lady was coming down the street and, farther up, a woman with a basket. Victoria became fidgety, she felt for her watch.

"Do you have to go now?" he asked. "Tell me something before you go, let me hear what you . . . I love you, now I've said it. So it will depend on your answer whether I . . . I'm completely in your power. What's your answer?"

Pause.

He lowered his head.

"No, don't tell me!" he begged her.

"Not here," she answered. "I'll let you know down there."

They started walking.

"People say you're going to marry that little girl, the girl you rescued, what's her name?"

"Camilla, you mean?"

"Camilla Seier. People say you're going to marry her."

"Really. Why do you ask about that? She isn't even grown up. I've been to her home, it's so rich and grand, a castle like your own; I've been there many times. Why, she's still a child."

"She's fifteen. I've met her, we've spent time together. I was very much taken with her. How lovely she is!"

"I'm not going to marry her," he said.

"No?"

He looked at her. His face twitched slightly.

"But why are you saying this now? Are you trying to draw my attention to someone else?"

She walked on with hurried steps and didn't reply. They found themselves outside the chamberlain's place. She took his hand and pulled him inside the gate and up the steps.

"I mustn't go in," he said, somewhat surprised.

She rang the bell and turned toward him, her breast heaving.

"I love you," she said. "Do you understand? You're the one I love."

Suddenly she pulled him quickly back down again, three or four steps, threw her arms around him and kissed him. She trembled against him.

"You're the one I love," she said.

The front door opened. She tore herself away and raced up the steps.

IV

It's almost morning; the day is breaking, a bluish, quivering September morning.

There is a faint soughing among the poplars in the garden. A window opens, a man leans out and starts humming. Coatless, he looks out on the world like a half-clothed madman who has gotten drunk on happiness during the night.

Suddenly he turns away from the window and looks at the door; someone has knocked. He calls, "Come in!" A man enters.

"Good morning!" he says to his visitor.

It is an elderly man; pale and furious, he's carrying a lamp in his hands, because it's not quite daylight yet.

"I must once again ask you, Mr. Møller, Mr. Johannes Møller, if you think this sort of thing is reasonable," the man stutters forth, indignant.

"No," Johannes answers, "you're right. I've written something, it came to me so easily; look, I've written all this, I've been lucky tonight. But now I've finished. So I opened the window and sang a bit."

"You were roaring," the man says. "In fact, it was the loudest singing I've ever heard. And in the middle of the night at that."

Johannes reaches for his papers on the table and takes a handful of sheets, large and small.

"Look here!" he cries. "I tell you, it has never gone so well before. It was like a long flash of lightning. I once saw a lightning flash run along a telegraph wire; I swear to God, it looked like a sheet of fire. That's how things have been moving along tonight. What shall I do? I can't believe you will go on bearing a grudge against me once you've heard the whole story. I sat here writing, I tell you, without stirring; I remembered about you and kept silent. Then, for a moment, it slipped my mind, my breast was about to burst; maybe I got up then, maybe I also got up once more in the course of the night and paced about the room a few times. I was so happy."

"I didn't hear you very much during the night," the man says. "But it's completely inexcusable of you to open the window at this hour and holler like that."

"Well, yes, it is inexcusable. But now I've given you an explanation. You see, I've never had a night like this. Something happened to me yesterday. I'm taking a walk and there, in the street, I meet my happiness—but listen, please: I meet my star and my happiness. And then, do you know, she kisses me. Her lips were so red and I love her, she kisses me and intoxicates me. Have your lips ever trembled so hard that you couldn't speak? I couldn't speak, my heart made my whole body shake. I raced home and fell asleep; I sat here, on this chair, and slept. When evening came I woke up. My soul was rocking up and down with excitement and I began to write. What I wrote? Here it is! I was carried away by a strange and glorious line of thought, the heavens were opened, it was like a warm summer's day for my soul; an angel offered me wine and I drank it, intoxicating wine which I drank out of a garnet cup. Did I hear the clock strike? Did I see the lamp burn itself out? I wish to God you'd understand! I lived it all afresh, one more time; I was again walking the street with my beloved and everybody turned to look at her. We walked in the park, we met the King, I lowered my hat to the ground before him for joy, and the King turned to look at her, at my beloved, because she is so tall and lovely. We walked downtown again, and all the school-children turned to look at her, because she is young and has a light-colored dress. When we came to a red brick house, we went in. I followed her up the steps and was about to kneel before her. Then she threw her arms around me and kissed me. This happened to me yesterday evening, as recently as that. If you were to ask me what I've written, I would say: I've written an endless song to joy, to happiness. It was as though happiness lay naked before me with a long, laughing throat and wanted to come to me."

"Hm, I really don't want to continue this conversation," the man says, annoyed and resigned. "I've spoken to you for the last time."

Johannes stops him at the door.

"Just a moment. Why, you should have seen yourself—it looked as though your face was wreathed in sunlight. I saw it the moment you turned around; it was the lamp, it threw a sun-fleck on your forehead. You weren't so angry anymore, I noticed. Well, I did open the window, and I sang too loud. I was everybody's happy brother. These things do happen sometimes. Common sense goes by the board. I ought to have considered that you were still asleep—"

"The whole town is still asleep."

"Yes, it's early. I would like to give you something. Will you accept this? It's silver, it was given to me. A little girl I once rescued gave it to me. There you are! It holds twenty cigarettes. You won't accept it? I see, you don't smoke; but you should really get into the habit. May I drop by tomorrow and offer my apologies? I would like to do something, ask your forgiveness. . . ."

"Good night."

"Good night. I'm going to bed now. I promise you I will. You won't hear another sound from here. And in the future I'll be more careful."

The man left.

Johannes suddenly reopened the door and added, "By the way,

I'll be leaving. I won't be disturbing you anymore, I'm leaving tomorrow. I forgot to tell you."

He did not leave. Several things detained him: there were errands to do, purchases to make, bills to be paid, and the evening and the morning passed. He rushed about like a lunatic.

At last he rang the bell at the chamberlain's. Was Victoria there?

Victoria was running some errands.

He explains that they, Miss Victoria and he, came from the same place, he would simply have liked to pay his respects if she'd been in—have permitted himself to pay his respects. There was a message he would have liked to send home. No matter.

Then he went downtown. Perhaps he would meet her, spot her, perhaps she was riding in a carriage. He wandered about until evening. Seeing her in front of the theater, he bowed to her, smiled and bowed, and she returned his greeting. He was about to go up to her—she was only a few steps away—when he noticed that she was not alone but with Otto, the chamberlain's son. He was in a lieutenant's uniform.

Perhaps she'll give me a hint, a small signal with her eyes, Johannes thought. She hurried into the theater, flushed and head bent, as if trying to hide.

Maybe he could see her inside? He bought a ticket and went in.

He knew where the chamberlain's box was—those wealthy people had a box, of course. There she sat in all her glory, looking about her. Did she look at him? Never!

When the act was over he looked for her in the vestibule. Again he bowed to her; she looked at him, a bit surprised, and nodded.

"You can get water over there," Otto said, pointing ahead.

They walked past.

Johannes gave them a long look. A strange dimness settled over his eyes. All these people were annoyed with him and jostled him; he begged their pardon mechanically and stayed put. There she disappeared.

When she returned he bowed deeply to her and said, "Pardon me, Miss . . ."

Otto answered him, screwing up his eyes.

"It's Johannes," she said, introducing him. "Don't you recognize him?"

"I suppose you want to know how things are at home," she went on, her face calm and beautiful. "I really don't know, but I believe all's well. Very good, I'll convey your kind regards to the Møllers."

"Thank you. Will you be leaving soon?"

"In a few days. Certainly, I'll convey your regards."

She nodded and walked away.

Again, Johannes followed her with his eyes until she had disappeared, then he went out. An endless wandering, a sad, heavy walk about the streets, up one and down another, helped while away the time. At ten o'clock he was waiting in front of the chamberlain's house. Soon the theaters would be closing and she would come. Perhaps he could open the carriage door and take his hat off, open the carriage door and bow to the ground.

At last, half an hour later, she came. Could he stand there by the gate and remind her again of his existence? He hurried up the street without looking right or left. He heard the gate at the chamberlain's being opened, the carriage driving in, and the gate being slammed to. Then he turned around.

He continued strolling up and down in front of the house for an hour. He wasn't expecting anyone and had no errand. Suddenly the gate is opened from the inside and Victoria steps into the street. She's bareheaded and has thrown only a shawl over her shoulders. She gives him a half-scared, half-embarrassed smile and, to start with, asks, "So you're walking about here, thinking?"

"No," he replies. "Thinking? No, I'm just walking about."

"I saw you pacing up and down outside and so I wanted to . . . I saw you from my window. I'll have to go right back."

"Thanks for coming, Victoria. I was in such despair a moment ago, but now it's over. I'm sorry I spoke to you in the theater; I'm afraid I've asked for you here at the chamberlain's too. I wanted to see you and find out what you meant, what you intend to do."

"Well," she said, "you must know that by now. I said

enough the day before yesterday to leave no room for misunderstanding."

"I'm still just as uncertain about everything."

"Let's say no more about it. I've said enough, I've said far too much, and I'm giving you pain. I love you, I wasn't lying the other day and I'm not lying now; but there are so many things that separate us. I'm very fond of you, I like talking with you, more than with anyone else, but . . . Hm, I dare not stay here any longer, they can see us from the windows. Johannes, there are so many reasons you don't know about, so you mustn't keep asking me to tell you what I mean. I've thought about it night and day; I mean what I've said. But it's impossible."

"What is impossible?"

"The whole thing. Everything. Listen, Johannes, don't force me to be proud for both of us."

"All right. Fine, you won't have to. But the fact is you fooled me the other day. You just happened to run across me in the street, you were in a good mood, and so—"

She turned to go in.

"Have I done something wrong?" he asked. His face was pale and unrecognizable. "I mean, what have I done to lose your . . . Have I committed some crime in these last two days and nights?"

"No. That's not it. It's just that I've thought it over; haven't you? It has been impossible all along, don't you know? I'm fond of you, I appreciate you—"

"And respect you."

She looks at him; his smile offends her and she continues more vehemently, "Good God, can't you understand that Papa would refuse you? Why do you force me to spell it out? You can figure that out by yourself. What would it all have come to? Am I not right?"

Pause.

"Yes," he says.

"Besides," she goes on, "there are so many reasons. . . . No, you really mustn't follow me to the theater again, you frightened me. You mustn't do that ever again."

"No," he says.

She takes his hand.

"Can't you come home for a while? I would very much look forward to that. How warm your hand is; I feel cold. No, now I must go. Good night."

"Good night," he answers.

The street stretched cold and gray before him, it looked like a belt of sand, an endless road to walk. He bumped into a boy selling old, lifeless roses; he called to him, took a rose, handed the boy a tiny gold five-krone piece, a gift, and went on. Shortly afterward he saw a group of children playing near an entrance. A ten-year-old boy sits quietly watching them; he has a pair of aged blue eyes that follow the game, hollow cheeks, and a square chin, and on his head he's wearing a canvas cap. It was the lining of a cap. This child wore a wig, a hair sickness had disfigured his head for good. And his soul was all withered, most likely.

He noticed all this, though he had no clear idea in which part of the city he found himself or where he was going. Then it began to rain but, not feeling it, he didn't open his umbrella, though he had been carrying it with him all day.

When he finally came to a square with some benches, he went and sat down. It was raining harder and harder; automatically, he opened the umbrella and stayed on. Soon after he was overcome by an irresistible drowsiness, his brain was enveloped in fog, and he closed his eyes and began to nod, dozing.

A while later he was awakened by the loud conversation of some passersby. He got up and rambled on. His brain had cleared, he remembered what had happened, every incident, even the boy to whom he gave five kroner for a rose. He imagined the rapture of the little gentleman when he discovered this strange coin among his pennies and realized it was not a twenty-five-øre coin, but a gold five-krone piece. God bless!

The other children had probably been driven away by the rain and were now continuing their games in the entrance, playing hopscotch and marbles. And the disfigured oldster of ten was watching them. Who knows, maybe he sat there being happy about something, maybe he had a doll in his little backstairs room, a jumping jack or a whirligig. Maybe he hadn't lost everything in life, leaving some hope in his withered soul.

A wispy, elegant lady suddenly turns up ahead of him. He gives a start and stops. No, he didn't know her. She had come

from a side street and was hurrying along, and she had no umbrella though it was pouring. He caught up with her, gave her a
glance, and walked past. How young and elegant she was! She
was getting wet and would catch a cold, but he didn't dare ap-
proach her. Instead, he closed his umbrella so she wouldn't be
the only one getting wet. It was past midnight when he got home.

A letter was lying on the table, a card—it was an invitation.
The Seiers would be delighted to have him come over tomorrow evening. He would meet people he knew, among others—
could he guess?—Victoria, the young lady from the Castle.
Kind regards.

He fell asleep in his chair. A couple of hours later he woke up
and felt cold. Half awake, half asleep, shivering all over and
weary from the day's adversities, he sat down at the table to answer the card, this invitation which he didn't intend to accept.

He wrote his answer and was about to take it down to the
mailbox. Suddenly it strikes him that Victoria was also invited.
Well, well. She hadn't said a word about it to him, she had been
afraid he would come, she didn't want to be seen with him there,
among strangers.

He tears up his letter and writes a new one, thanking them
for the invitation: he would be glad to come. Repressed anger
makes his hand tremble, he's seized by a strange, gleeful indignation. Why shouldn't he go? Why should he hide? Enough.

He's carried away by his violent emotion. With one twitch, he
tears a handful of leaves off his wall calendar, putting himself a
week ahead of time. He imagines he's happy about something,
exceedingly delighted; he wants to savor this moment, light a
pipe, sit down in his chair and gloat. The pipe is in very bad
shape, he looks in vain for a knife, a scraper; suddenly he jerks
one hand off the corner clock to clean his pipe with. This piece
of destruction is a feast to the eye, it makes him laugh inwardly,
and he peers about him for more things to throw into confusion.

Time goes by. At long last he throws himself on the bed fully
dressed, in his wet clothes, and falls asleep.

When he woke up the day was already far advanced. It was
still raining, the streets were wet. His head was in turmoil, frag-
ments of his dreams became mixed up with yesterday's experiences, but he wasn't running a fever. On the contrary, his

temperature had tapered off, a coolness was coming his way, as
if he had been wandering all night in a sultry forest and now
found himself in the vicinity of a lake.

There is a knock at the door, the mailman brings him a letter.
He opens it, takes a look at it, reads it and has difficulty figur-
ing it out. It was from Victoria, a note, a half-sheet: she had
forgotten to tell him that she was going to the Seiers' this evening, she hoped to see him there; she would give him a better
explanation, ask him to forget her, to take it like a man. Sorry
about the wretched paper. Kind regards.

He went out, had something to eat, came back home, and finally sent his regrets to the Seiers. He couldn't make it; he
would take a rain check and come some other time, tomorrow
evening, for example.

He sent the letter by messenger.

V

Fall came. Victoria had gone home, and the small, out-of-the-
way street lay there as before, with its houses and its silence. In
Johannes' room the lamp burned through the night. It was
lighted in the evening when the stars came out and was put out
at the crack of dawn. He was working tirelessly, writing his big
book.

Weeks and months passed; he was alone and called on nobody, he never went to the Seiers' anymore. Often his imagination played crazy tricks on him, messing up his book with
irrelevant fancies that later had to be erased and trashed. This
set him back a great deal. A sudden noise in the nocturnal
silence, the rumble of a carriage in the street, would give his
thinking a jolt and throw it off course.

Make way for this carriage in the street, watch out!

Why? Why should one watch out for this carriage? It rolled
past, by now it may be at the corner. Perhaps a man is in the way;
coatless and hatless, he stands there bent forward, meeting the
carriage head-on—he'll be run over, irreparably injured, killed.
The man wants to die, that's his affair. He no longer buttons his
shirt, has stopped lacing his shoes in the morning, and goes about

with everything open, his chest bare and emaciated; he is to
die. . . . A man lying at death's door wrote a letter to his friend,
a note, a small request. The man died, leaving this letter. It had
a date and a signature, it was written with capital and small letters, though he who wrote it was to die within the hour. It was so
strange. He had even made the usual flourish under his name.
And an hour later he was dead. . . . There was another man.
He lies alone in a small room, painted blue and with wood pan-
eling. So what? Oh, nothing. In the whole wide world, he's the
one who is going to die. Preoccupied by this, he thinks about it to
the point of exhaustion. He can see it is evening, that the clock on
the wall says eight, and he can't figure out why it doesn't strike.
The clock doesn't strike. Actually, it's a few minutes past eight
and it keeps on ticking, but it doesn't strike. Poor man, his brain
is already going to sleep, the clock has struck and he didn't notice. He pricks a hole in his mother's picture on the wall—what
does he want with this picture now, and why should it remain
whole when he's gone? His weary eyes fall on the flowerpot on
the table and, stretching out his hand, he slowly and deliber-
ately pulls the large flowerpot to the floor, where it goes to
pieces. Why should it stand there, whole? Then he throws his
amber cigarette holder out the window. What does he need that
for anymore? It seems quite obvious that it doesn't have to be
left behind. And in a week the man was dead. . . .

Johannes stands up and paces the floor, up and down. His
neighbor in the next room wakes up, his snoring has stopped
and a sigh, a pained groan, is heard. Johannes tiptoes over to
the table and sits down again. The wind whistles through the
poplars outside his window, making him feel cold. The old poplars are stripped of their leaves and look like miserable freaks
of nature; some gnarled branches grinding against the wall
produce a creaking sound, like a wooden machine, a cracked
stamping mill that runs and runs.

He casts his eyes down at his papers and reads them through.
To be sure, his imagination has led him astray again. He has
nothing to do with death or with a passing carriage. He's writing
about a garden, about a lush, green garden near his home, the
Castle garden. That is what he's writing about. It's dead and
covered with snow now, and yet that is what he's writing about,

and it isn't winter with snow at all, but spring with fragrance and mild breezes. And it's evening. The lake below is still and deep, it's like a leaden sea; there's a scent of lilacs, hedge after hedge is in bud or green with foliage, and the air is so still that you can hear the blackcock's mating call across the bay. In one of the garden walks stands Victoria, alone, dressed in white, with twenty summers behind her. There she stands. Her figure is taller than the tallest rosebushes; she's looking out over the lake to the woods, toward the sleeping mountains in the distance. She appears like a white spirit in the middle of the green garden. Footsteps are heard from the road, she takes a few steps forward, down to the hidden pavilion, leans her elbows on the garden wall and looks downward. The man on the road doffs his hat, nearly sweeping the ground with it, and nods to her. She nods back. The man looks about him; seeing no spies around, he takes a few steps toward the wall. She falls back, crying, No, no! She also wards him off with her hand. Victoria, he says, what you once told me was absolutely true, I shouldn't have deluded myself, because it is impossible. Yes, she replies, but what then do you want? He's now quite close to her, only the wall separates them as he answers, What I want? Well, you see, I just want to stand here a minute. It's the last time. I want to be as close to you as possible; now I'm not so far away! She is silent. The minute passes. Good night, he says, and again he doffs his hat and nearly sweeps the ground with it. Good night, she answers. And he leaves without looking back. . . .

What did he have to do with death? He crumples the scribbled sheet and tosses it over to the stove, where also other papers covered with writing are waiting to be burned—mere fleeting fancies of an overflowing imagination. And he writes again about the man in the road, a wandering gentleman who gave his greeting and then said good-bye when his minute was up. Remaining in the garden was the young girl of twenty, dressed in white. She wouldn't have him, well and good. But he had stood by the wall behind which she lived. He was that close to her once.

Again weeks and months went by and spring came around. The snow was already gone, and the expanse of space, from the sun to the moon, resounded with a roar as of released waters. The swallows had come back, and in the woods outside the city there awakened a bustling life of all kinds of jumping creatures, and of birds chirping in strange tongues. A fresh, sweetish smell rose from the earth.

Johannes' work has occupied him all winter. The dry branches of the poplars had creaked against the wall like a sailor's chantey night and day; now spring has come, the storms are past, and the stamping mill has ground to a halt.

He opens the window and looks out; the street is already quiet though it's not yet midnight, the stars twinkle from a cloudless sky: tomorrow promises to be a clear, warm day. He can hear the rumble of the city, which mingles with the ceaseless roar from afar. Suddenly there is the piercing sound of a railroad whistle, the signal of the night train; it sounds like a lone cock crow in the silent night. The time has come for work—this train whistle has been like a signal to him all winter.

And he closes the window and sits down at the table again. He tosses aside the books he has been reading and gets out his papers. He picks up his pen.

His long work is nearly finished, only the concluding chapter is lacking, a sort of salute from a departing ship, and it is already there, in his head:

A gentleman sits in a wayside inn; he is just passing through on a long, long journey. His hair and beard are gray, the years have left their mark on him; but he's still big and strong and hardly as old as he looks. His carriage is outside, the horses are resting, the coachman is happy and contented; he has been wined and dined by the stranger. When the gentleman checks in, the innkeeper recognizes his name and bows to him, doing him great honor. Who lives at the Castle now? the gentleman asks. The captain, the innkeeper replies, he's very rich; the lady is kind to everyone. To everyone? the gentleman asks himself, smiling mysteriously, even to me? And he starts writing something on a piece of paper, and when it's finished he reads it through; it's a poem, serene and sad, but with many bitter words. Afterward, however, he tears the paper up, and he continues to sit there tearing the paper up even more. Then there is a knock on his door and a woman dressed in yellow enters. She lifts her veil, it's the mistress of the

Castle, Lady Victoria. She has a majestic air about her. The gentleman rises abruptly, his dark soul illumined as by a spear fisher's flash the same instant. You are so kind to all, he says bitterly, you even come to me. Instead of answering, she simply stands there gazing at him, her face turning crimson. What do you want? he asks, just as bitterly as before. Have you come to remind me of the past? If so, gracious lady, it will be the last time, for now I'm leaving forever. The young mistress of the Castle still doesn't answer, but her lips quaver. If it isn't enough for you that I acknowledged my folly once, he says, then listen, I'll do it again: My heart was yours, but I wasn't worthy of you. Are you satisfied now? He continues with increasing vehemence: You refused me, you took another; I was a peasant, a bear, a barbarian who in his youth strayed onto the royal preserve! But then the gentleman flops down in a chair, sobbing and pleading, Oh, go away! Forgive me and go! By now all color has faded from the lady's face. Then she says, articulating her words slowly and clearly: I love you; do not misunderstand me anymore, you are the one I love. Good-bye! And that was the young mistress of the Castle; she hid her face in her hands and made a quick exit. . . .

He puts down his pen and leans back. Good, period, the end. There lies the book, all those pages covered with writing, nine months' labor. The completion of his work gives him a warm thrill of satisfaction. And as he sits there looking through the window at the crack of dawn, his head throbs and buzzes and his mind goes on working. His heart is full, and his brain is like an unharvested wild garden in which vapors are rising from the earth.

In some mysterious way he has come to a deep, deserted valley where no living thing can be found. In the distance, alone and abandoned, an organ is playing. He walks closer, he examines it; the organ is bleeding, blood flows from its side as it plays. Farther on, he comes to a market square. It is completely empty, no trees can be seen and no sounds are heard, it's simply an empty square. But there are footprints in the sand, and the last words spoken there still seem to hover in the air, so it was abandoned very recently. He's caught up in an eerie sensation: these words hovering in the air over the square frighten him, they close in on him, oppress him. He fends them off, but they come back—

they are not words but old men, a group of old men dancing; he can see them now. Why are they dancing, and why are they not the least bit joyful when they dance? A cold wind blows from this company of old men; they don't see him, they're blind, and when he calls to them they don't hear him, they are dead. He wanders east, toward the sun, and comes to a mountain. A voice cries, Are you near a mountain? Yes, he replies, I'm standing near a mountain. Then the voice says, The mountain you're standing at is my foot; I'm lying bound at the ends of the earth, come and release me! And so he sets off for the ends of the earth. At a bridge he is waylaid by a man who collects shadows; the man is formed of musk. He is seized by a chilling horror at the sight of this man, who wants to take away his shadow. He spits at him and threatens him with clenched fists, but the man remains motionless, waiting for him. Turn around! cries a voice behind him. He turns and sees a head rolling down the road, showing him the way. It is a human head, and now and then it gives a soundless laugh. He follows it. It rolls for days and nights and he follows it; at the seashore it slips into the ground and hides. He wades out into the sea and dives. He's standing at a huge gate, where he meets a large barking fish. Its neck has a mane, and it barks at him like a dog. Behind the fish stands Victoria. He stretches out his hands toward her; she has no clothes on and gives him a smile, and a gale blows through her hair. Then he calls to her, he hears his own scream—and wakes up.

Johannes gets up and goes over to the window. It is almost daylight, and in the little mirror on the windowsill he can see that his temples are flushed. He puts out the lamp and reads once more, by the gray light of day, the last page of his book. Then he goes to bed.

By late afternoon that same day Johannes had paid the rent, delivered his manuscript and left town. He had gone abroad, no one knew where.

VI

The big book appeared—a kingdom, a small world astir with moods, voices, and visions. It was sold, read, and put away. A

few months went by; when fall came Johannes launched another book. What now? Suddenly his name was on everybody's
lips, he was lucky; the new book was written far away, at a
great distance from the goings-on at home, and it was still and
strong, like wine:

Dear reader! This is the story of Didrik and Iselin. Written in the
good days, a time of small sorrows when everything was easy to
bear, written with the best will in the world about Didrik, whom
God smote with love.

Johannes was in foreign parts, nobody knew where. More
than a year passed before anyone learned about it.

"I think there is somebody at the door," says the old miller one
evening.

He and his wife sit quietly and listen.

"No, there's no one," she says. "It's ten o'clock, almost
nighttime."

Several minutes go by.

Then there is a hard, resolute knock, as if someone needed to
pluck up courage for it. The miller opens the door. The young
lady from the Castle stands outside.

"Don't be alarmed, it's only me," she says, smiling timorously. She steps in; she's offered a chair but doesn't sit down.
She has only a shawl over her head and small, low shoes on her
feet, though it isn't yet spring and the roads aren't dry.

"I only wanted to let you know that the Lieutenant will be
coming this spring," she says. "The Lieutenant, my fiancé. And
he may be hunting woodcock out this way. I just wanted to let
you know, so you wouldn't be worried."

The miller and his wife look at the young lady in surprise.
This was the first time they had ever been warned when visitors
at the Castle would go hunting in field and forest. They thank
her humbly; how very kind of her!

Victoria steps back to the door.

"That's all. You people were old, I thought there would be
no harm in letting you know."

"How nice of you to think of us!" the miller says. "And now
you've gotten your feet all wet, in those small shoes."

"No, the road is dry," she says shortly. "I was taking this walk anyway. Good night."

"Good night."

She unlatches the door and steps out. In the doorway she turns around and asks, "By the way, have you heard from Johannes?"

"No, not a word. Thanks for asking. Nothing."

"He'll be coming soon, no doubt. I thought you might have some news from him."

"No, not since last spring. Johannes is supposed to be abroad."

"Yes, abroad. He's doing well. He says in a book that he's living in a time of small sorrows. So he must be doing well."

"Ah, God knows. We're waiting for him; but he doesn't write to us, or to anyone. We can only wait for him."

"He's probably doing better where he is, since his sorrows are small. Well, that's his business. I only wanted to know if he would be coming home this spring. Good night again."

"Good night."

The miller and his wife follow her out. They watch her returning to the Castle, head held high, stepping over the puddles on the soggy road in her tiny shoes.

A couple of days later there is a letter from Johannes. He will be home in just over a month, after finishing yet another book. He has had a nice long spell of fruitful work, a new volume was nearly completed, his brain had been teeming with all the world's life. . . .

The miller sets out for the Castle. On the way he finds a handkerchief; it's marked with Victoria's initials, she must have dropped it the other evening.

The young lady is upstairs, but a maid offers to take the message—what was it about?

The miller declines to say. He prefers to wait.

At last the young lady appears. "I understand you wish to speak to me," she says, opening the door to a room.

The miller walks in, hands her the handkerchief and says, "We've had a letter from Johannes."

Her face lights up for an instant, a fleeting instant. "Thank you," she says. "Yes, the handkerchief is mine."

"He'll be coming home," the miller goes on in a near whisper.

Her face assumes a chilly expression. "Speak up, miller; who's coming?" she says.

"Johannes."

"Johannes. Well, what then?"

"Oh, it was just . . . We figured I ought to let you know. My wife and I discussed it, and she thought so too. You asked the other day if he would be coming home this spring. Well, he's coming."

"That must make you very happy," the young lady says. "When is he coming?"

"In a month."

"I see. And there wasn't anything else?"

"No. We just thought that since you asked . . . No, there wasn't anything else. Only this."

The miller had again lowered his voice.

She sees him out. In the hallway they meet her father, and she says to him in passing, loudly and nonchalantly, "The miller tells me that Johannes is coming home. You remember Johannes, don't you?"

And the miller walks out through the Castle gate, promising himself never, never again to be a fool and listen to his wife when she claimed to understand hidden things. And he means to let her know.

VII

At one time he had wanted to cut down the slender rowan tree by the millpond to make a fishing rod; now many years had passed, and the tree had become thicker than his arm. He looked at it in wonder and walked on.

Along the river, the impenetrable jungle of ferns still flourished, a veritable forest through which the cattle had trampled regular paths, now arched over by the overhanging fern fronds. He fought his way through the thicket as in his childhood days, swimming with his hands and feeling his way with his feet. Insects and crawling things fled before the enormous man.

Up by the granite quarry he found blackthorn, white anemones and violets. He picked a few, their familiar fragrance called him back to days gone by. The hills of the neighboring parish showed blue in the distance, and across the bay the cuckoo started calling.

He sat down; shortly he began humming. Then he heard footsteps on the path.

It was evening, the sun had set, but the heat still quivered in the air. An infinite stillness hovered over the woods, the hills, and the bay. A woman was coming up toward the quarry. It was Victoria. She was carrying a basket.

Johannes stood up, bowed, and made as if to go.

"I didn't mean to disturb you," she said. "I just wanted to get some flowers."

He didn't answer. And it didn't occur to him that she had all the flowers in the world in her garden.

"I've brought a basket to put the flowers in," she went on. "But perhaps I won't find any. It's because of the party, we need them for the table. We're going to have a party."

"Here are white anemones and violets," he said. "Higher up one can usually find avens. But it may be too early in the year for those."

"You're paler than the last time we met," she remarked. "That was more than two years ago. You've been away, I hear. I've read your books."

He still didn't answer. It occurred to him that he might just say, "Well, my young lady, have a good evening!" and go. From where he stood it was one step down to the next stone, from there one more to her, whereupon he could withdraw as if it were the most natural thing in the world. She was standing directly in his way. She had on a yellow dress and a red hat, she was mysterious and beautiful; her throat was bare.

"I'm blocking your path," he murmured, stepping down. He tried hard not to betray any emotion.

There was now only one step separating them. She made no move to get out of his way, but simply stood there. They looked each other squarely in the face. Suddenly she blushed crimson, dropped her eyes and stepped aside; her face assumed an expression of helplessness, but she smiled.

Having walked past her, he stopped, struck by her mournful smile; his heart again flew to her and he said at random, "Well, you must've been in town many times since then? Since that time? . . . Now I remember where there used to be flowers in the old days: on the knoll by your flagpole."

She turned toward him; he was surprised to see that her face had turned pale with emotion.

"Will you come to us that evening?" she said. "Will you come to the party? We're going to have a party," she went on, coloring up again. "Some city people are coming. It will be quite soon, I'll let you know more later. What do you say?"

He didn't answer. That was no party for him, he didn't belong to the Castle crowd.

"You mustn't say no. You won't be bored. I've given it some thought—I have a surprise for you."

Pause.

"You can't give me any more surprises," he replied.

She bit her lip; a disconsolate smile again passed across her face.

"What do you want me to do?" she said listlessly.

"I don't want you to do anything, Miss Victoria. I was sitting here on a stone, I'm willing to move."

"I came here, alas, after wandering about at home all day. I could have walked along the river, by another path, then I wouldn't have ended up just here—"

"My dear young lady, this place is yours, not mine."

"I hurt you once, Johannes, I would like to make up for it, put it right. I do, indeed, have a surprise which I think . . . that is, which I hope you'll be pleased with. I can't say more. But I must ask you to show up this time."

"If it will give you any pleasure, I shall come."

"Will you?"

"Yes, and thank you for your kindness."

When he reached the woods he turned and looked back. She had sat down; the basket was beside her. He didn't go home but continued to wander up and down the road. A legion of thoughts were battling inside him. A surprise? That's what she said, just a moment ago, her voice was trembling. An intense, nervous joy wells up in him, setting his heart thumping, and he feels as though he's walking on air. And was it mere coincidence that she was dressed in yellow today? He had looked at her hand, where she once wore a ring—there wasn't any ring.

An hour goes by. He was enveloped by the exhalations of field and forest; they mingled with his breath and entered his heart. He sat down, lay back with his hands folded under his head and listened for a while to the song of the cuckoo across the bay. An ardent warbling quavered in the air about him.

So it had happened to him once again! When she came up to him in the quarry in her yellow dress and blood-red hat, she looked like a roving butterfly, moving from stone to stone and settling before him. "I didn't mean to disturb you," she said and smiled; her smile was red, her whole face lighted up, she scattered stars about her. Her throat had acquired some delicate blue veins, and the few freckles below her eyes gave her a warm complexion. She was in her twentieth year.

A surprise? What did she mean to do? Maybe she would show him his books, take out those two or three volumes to make him happy because she had bought them and cut the pages? Here you are, a crumb of comfort and attention! Do not refuse my humble offering!

He jumped to his feet and remained motionless. Victoria was coming back, her basket empty.

"You didn't find any flowers?" he asked absently.

"No, I gave up. I wasn't even looking, I just sat there."

"While I remember," he said, "you mustn't go around thinking you've hurt me in some way. You have nothing to make up for with any kind of comfort."

"I don't?" she answered, taken aback. She thought it over, looking at him and wondering. "I don't? I thought that time . . . I didn't want you to bear a grudge against me forever because of what happened."

"But I don't bear a grudge against you."

She thinks a while longer. Suddenly she draws herself up. "Then all's well," she says. "Oh, I should have known. It didn't leave enough of an impression on you for that. Very well, we won't say any more about it."

"No, let's not. My impressions matter as little to you now as before."

"Good-bye," she said. "Good-bye for now."

"Good-bye," he replied.

They went their separate ways. He stopped and turned around. There she was, moving along. He stretched out his hands and whispered, speaking tender words to himself: "I don't bear a grudge against you, oh, no, I don't; I love you still, love you. . . ."

"Victoria!" he called.

She heard him, gave a start and turned, but continued walking.

A few days went by. Johannes was extremely restless and couldn't work or sleep; he spent almost all his time in the woods. He climbed the big pine-clad knoll where the Castle flagpole stood; the flag was flying. They had also hoisted the flag on the Castle's round tower.

A strange excitement laid hold of him. Visitors were expected at the Castle, they were going to celebrate.

The afternoon was calm and warm; the river throbbed like a pulse as it flowed through the steamy landscape. A steamer came gliding into port, leaving a fan of white streaks in the bay. And now four carriages were leaving the Castle yard, heading for the pier.

The ship came alongside, gentlemen and ladies stepped ashore and took their seats in the carriages. Then salvos of gunfire came from the Castle; two men with sporting guns stood in the round tower loading and firing, loading and firing. When they had let fly twenty-one rounds, the carriages rolled in through the Castle gate and the firing ceased.

Yes, indeed, there would be festivities at the Castle; the visitors were received with flags and salutes. In the carriages there were some military gentlemen—Otto, the Lieutenant, among them perhaps.

Johannes came down from the knoll and went home. He was overtaken by a man from the Castle, who stopped him. The man had a letter in his cap, he had been sent by Miss Victoria and requested an answer.

Johannes read the letter, his heart going pit-a-pat. Victoria was inviting him all the same, she wrote in a cordial manner and asked him to come. This was the one time she wanted to invite him. Reply by the messenger.

A wonderful, unexpected happiness had befallen him; the blood rose to his head and he answered the man that he would come, yes, he would come presently, thanks.

"There you are!" He handed the messenger a ridiculously large coin and raced home to get dressed.

VIII

For the first time in his life he walked through the Castle gate and climbed the stairs to the second floor. A buzz of voices reached him from inside, his heart was thumping, he knocked and went in.

He was met by the still youthful hostess, who greeted him amiably and shook his hand. Very glad to see him, she remembered him from when he was only so high, and now he was a great man. . . . It looked as though she would have liked to say something more, she held his hand for a long time and gave him a searching look.

The host also appeared and gave him his hand. As his wife had said, a great man in more than one sense. A famous man. Very pleased . . .

He was introduced to gentlemen and ladies, to the chamberlain, who was wearing his decorations, to the chamberlain's wife, to a neighboring landowner, to Otto, the Lieutenant. He didn't see Victoria.

Some time went by. Victoria came in, pale, diffident; she was leading a young girl by the hand. They made a tour of the room, greeting one and all, exchanging a few words with each. They stopped before Johannes.

Victoria smiled and said, "Look, here is Camilla, isn't that a surprise? You know each other."

She observed them both briefly, then left the room.

For a moment Johannes stood rooted to the spot, rigid and confused. Here was the surprise! Victoria had kindly provided a surrogate. Hey, you folks, go and tie the knot! Spring is in bloom, the sun is shining; open the windows if you like, there is perfume in the garden, and the starlings are pairing off in the birch-tops. Why don't you talk to each other? Laugh, won't you!

"Yes, we know each other," Camilla said candidly. "It was here you fished me out of the water that time."

She was young and fair, lively, dressed in pink, in her seventeenth year. Johannes clenched his teeth and laughed and joked. Gradually her cheerful words really began to revive him; they talked for a long time, his palpitation calmed down. She had kept from her childhood the charming habit of tilting her head and listening expectantly when he said something. He recognized her, all right; she was no surprise to him.

Victoria came in again; taking the Lieutenant's arm, she pulled him along and said to Johannes, "Do you know Otto— my fiancé? I suppose you remember him."

The gentlemen remembered each other. They speak the necessary words, make the necessary bows, and part company. Johannes and Victoria are left by themselves. "Was that the surprise?" he says.

"Yes," she replies, pained and impatient. "I did the best I could, I didn't know what else to do. Now, don't be unreasonable, rather say thank you; I could see you were pleased."

"Thank you. Yes, I was pleased."

A hopeless despair descended on him, his face turned deathly pale. If she had ever hurt him, he was now amply compensated and comforted. He was sincerely grateful to her.

"And I notice you're wearing your ring today," he said in a muffled voice. "Now, don't take it off again."

Pause.

"No, now I'm not likely to take it off again," she replied.

Their eyes met. His lips quivering, he turned his head in the direction of the Lieutenant and said, in a hoarse, gruff voice, "You have good taste, Victoria. He's a handsome man. His epaulets give him a pair of shoulders."

She retorted with great composure, "No, he's not handsome. But he is a well-bred man. That counts for something too."

"That was for me. Thank you!" Laughing aloud, he added rudely, "And he's got money in his pockets, that counts for even more."

She abruptly walked away.

He drifted about from wall to wall like an outcast. Camilla spoke to him, asking him about something, but he neither heard nor answered. She said something again, touching his arm as she repeated her question, but to no avail. "Ah, he's busy thinking," she cried, laughing. "He's thinking, he's thinking!"

Victoria heard her and said, "He wants to be left alone. He sent me away too." But suddenly she stepped right up to him and said aloud, "No doubt you're trying to dream up an apology. Don't trouble yourself. On the contrary, I owe you an apology for sending you the invitation so late. It showed great negligence on my part. I forgot about you till the very last moment, I nearly forgot about you altogether. But I hope you will forgive me, I had so many things on my mind."

He stared at her, speechless. Even Camilla seemed amazed as she looked from one to the other. Victoria was standing directly in front of them, a satisfied look on her cold, pale face. She had had her revenge.

"That's our young gallants for you," she said to Camilla. "We mustn't expect too much of them. Over there sits my fiancé talking about moose hunting, and here stands the poet absorbed in thought. . . . Say something, poet!"

He gave a start; the veins in his temples turned blue.

"Very well. You are asking me to say something? Very well."

"Oh, don't strain yourself."

She made as if to leave.

"To come straight to the point," he said slowly, with a smile, though his voice trembled, "to start with the crux of the matter: Have you been in love recently, Miss Victoria?"

For a few seconds there was total silence; all three of them could hear their hearts pounding. Camilla offered timorously, "Victoria is in love with her fiancé, of course. She's just become engaged, don't you know?"

The doors to the dining room were thrown open.

Johannes found his place and stopped in front of it. The whole table was rocking up and down before his eyes; he saw a great many people and heard a murmur of voices.

"Yes, that's your place, so please," the hostess said amiably. "If only everybody would sit down at last."

"Pardon me!" Victoria said of a sudden from just behind him. He stepped aside.

She took his card and moved it several places, seven places down, next to an old man who had once been a tutor at the Castle and had a reputation as a tippler. She brought another card back and sat down.

He stood there watching it all. The hostess, feeling uncomfortable, made herself busy on the other side of the table and avoided his glance.

Shaken and more bewildered than ever, he went to his new place; one of Ditlef's city friends, a young man with diamond studs in his shirtfront, moved into the original one. On his left sat Victoria, on his right Camilla.

The dinner began.

The old tutor remembered Johannes as a child, and a conversation started up between them. He related that he too had pursued the art of poetry as a young man; the manuscripts were still lying around, he would let Johannes read them some day. And now he had been summoned to this house on its day of rejoicing so he could share in the family's happiness at Victoria's engagement. The master and mistress of the house had prepared this surprise for him for old times' sake.

"I haven't read any of your things," he said. "If I want to read something, I read my own things; I have both poems and stories in my drawer. They are to be published after my death; I do want the public to know who I was, after all. We who've been in the profession somewhat longer aren't in such a hurry to bring everything to the printer's as they are nowadays, alas. Skoal!"

The dinner goes forward. The host taps his glass and rises. His lean, aristocratic face is quick with emotion, and he gives an impression of being extremely happy. Johannes bends his head very low. His glass is empty and no one offers him anything; he fills it to the brim himself and again lets his head droop. Now it would come!

The speech was nice and long and was received with a good deal of noisy cheer; the engagement was announced. Lots of good wishes for the host's daughter and the chamberlain's son poured in from every corner of the table.

Johannes emptied his glass.

A few minutes later his agitation is gone, his composure has returned; the champagne burns with a low flame in his veins. Then he hears the chamberlain speak, followed by renewed shouts of bravo and hurrah and the clinking of glasses. He casts a glance to where Victoria is sitting; she's pale, seems anguished, and doesn't look up. Camilla, however, nods to him and smiles, and he nods back.

The tutor goes on talking beside him. "It's beautiful, beautiful, when two people find one another. That was not my lot. I was a young student, good prospects, great gifts; my father had an ancient name, a large house, wealth, many, many ships. So it would be no exaggeration to say I had *very* good prospects. She was young too, and high up in society. Well, I come to her and open my heart. '*No,*' she says. Can you understand her? No, she didn't want to, she said. I did what I could, got on with my work and took it like a man. Then came my father's lean years, the shipwrecks, the surety claims, in short, he went bankrupt. And what did I do? Took it like a man again. But now the girl, the one I'm talking about, no longer shuns me. No, she comes back, looks me up in town. What was she after, you're going to ask. I was poor, with only a small teaching job, all my prospects gone and my poems put away in a drawer. But now she came and wanted to. Yes, she wanted to!"

The tutor looked at Johannes and asked, "Can you figure her out?"

"And then it was you who didn't want to?"

"Could I? I ask. Penniless, naked and exposed, with a teaching post, tobacco in my pipe on Sundays only—what do you imagine? I couldn't do that to her. I'm simply asking, can you figure her out?"

"And what became of her afterward?"

"Good Lord, you're not answering my question. She married a captain. That was the following year. A captain of artillery. Skoal!"

"Certain women, they say, are looking for a chance to exercise their compassion," Johannes remarked. "If the man does well, they hate him and feel superfluous; if he does poorly and buckles under, they crow and say, 'Here I am.' "

"But why didn't she accept me when things were going well? I had the prospects of a demigod."

"Well, she wanted to wait until you were brought low. God knows."

"But I was not brought low. Never. I kept my pride and turned her down. What do you say to that?"

Johannes didn't answer.

"But perhaps you're right," the old tutor said. "By God and all his angels, you're right in what you're saying," he exclaimed, suddenly animated, and took another drink. "In the end she took an old captain; she nurses him, cuts up his meat for him, and wears the pants in the house. A captain of artillery."

Johannes looked up. Victoria sat with her glass in her hand, staring in his direction. She raised her glass high in the air. He felt a jolt go through him, and he too picked up his glass. His hand was shaking.

Then, bursting into laughter, she called aloud to his neighbor; it was the tutor's name she called.

Humiliated, Johannes put down his glass, giving a perplexed, empty smile. Everybody had had their eyes on him.

The old tutor was moved to tears by this friendly attention from his pupil. He quickly emptied his glass.

"And here I am, an old man now," he continued, "here I am, walking the earth alone and unknown. That became my lot. No one knows what I've got in me, but no one has heard me grumble. By the way, are you familiar with the turtledove? Isn't it the turtledove, with its great penchant for mourning, that muddies the clear, bright spring water before drinking?"

"I don't know."

"No, indeed. It is, though. And I do the same. I didn't get the one I was supposed to have; still, my life is anything but lacking in pleasures. But I muddy them up. I always muddy them up. Then the disappointment can't get the better of me afterward. Look at Victoria there. She just drank a toast with me. I used to be her tutor, now she's getting married and I'm happy for her; it makes me feel a truly personal happiness, as if she were my own daughter. Some day, perhaps, I'll tutor her children. Yes, life still offers quite a few pleasures, it certainly does. But what you said about compassion and women and buckling under— the more I think about it, the more I think you are right. God knows you are. . . . Excuse me a moment."

He rose, picked up his glass and went up to Victoria. He was already a bit unsteady on his legs and walked with a marked stoop.

There were some more speeches; the Lieutenant spoke, the neighboring landowner raised his glass to the fair sex, to the lady of the house. Suddenly the gentleman with the diamond studs rose and mentioned Johannes' name. He had received permission for what he was doing: he wished to salute the young poet on behalf of youth. His words, spoken in a spirit of pure friendship, were offered as a well-meant thank-you from his contemporaries, full of recognition and admiration.

Johannes could barely believe his own ears. "Is he giving a speech for me?" he whispered to the tutor.

"Yes," the tutor replied. "He forestalled me. I was going to do it myself; Victoria asked me to already this afternoon."

"Who asked you, did you say?"

The tutor stared at him. "Nobody," he answered.

During the speech all eyes turned toward Johannes; even the host nodded to him, and the chamberlain's wife put on her pince-nez and gazed at him. When the speech was over, they all drank to him.

"Now you must return the favor," the tutor said. "He was giving that speech for you. It ought to have fallen to an older member of the profession. Besides, I didn't at all agree with him. Not at all."

Johannes cast a glance along the table toward Victoria. It was she who had made the gentleman with the diamond studs speak; why had she done it? At first she had approached someone else, she had harbored the thought already early in the day. Why? Now she sat looking down, with a facial expression that betrayed nothing.

Suddenly his eyes become misted with a deep and intense emotion; he could have thrown himself at her feet and thanked her, yes, thanked her. He would do so later, after dinner.

Camilla was talking right and left, her face all smiles. She was contented, her seventeen years had brought her nothing but pure joy. She nodded repeatedly to Johannes and made signs to him to stand up.

He stood up.

He spoke briefly, his voice deep and trembling with emotion: The festivity with which the family was celebrating a happy event had also brought him, though a complete outsider, out of his obscurity. He wished to thank the person who had originally come up with this amiable idea, as well as the one who had said so many agreeable things about him. Nor could he omit expressing his appreciation for the kindness with which the entire company had listened to his—the outsider's—praises. The one and only claim he had to be present on this occasion was that he happened to be the son of the Castle's neighbor in the woods—

"Yes!" Victoria suddenly cried, her eyes blazing.

Everyone turned to look at her. Her cheeks were flushed and her breast heaving. Johannes paused. An embarrassing silence ensued.

"Victoria!" her father said, astonished.

"Go on!" she cried. "That is your only claim, but go on talking!" Then her eyes suddenly went dead, she began smiling helplessly and shaking her head. Afterward she turned to her father and said, "I only meant to exaggerate. After all, he stands there exaggerating himself. I didn't mean to interrupt. . . ."

Johannes listened to this explanation and found a way out; his heart was beating audibly. He noticed that the hostess was looking at Victoria with tears in her eyes and with infinite forbearance.

Yes, he said, he had exaggerated; Miss Victoria was right. She had kindly reminded him that he was not only the neighbor's son but also the Castle children's playmate from early on, and it was to this latter circumstance that he owed his presence here now. He thanked her, she was right. He belonged to this place; the Castle woods were once his entire world, and behind them, in the blue distance, was the unknown—fairyland. But in those days he would often be asked by Ditlef and Victoria to come along on an excursion or to play a game—these were the great experiences of his childhood. After thinking it over, he had to admit that those times had meant more to him than anyone knew, and if it was true—as had just been said—that what he wrote occasionally *sparkled,* it was because his memories of that time fired him; it was a reflection of the happiness his two friends had given him in his childhood. Therefore they too had a large share in what he accomplished. And so, to the general good wishes on the occasion of the engagement, he would like to add his personal thanks to both of the Castle children for those good childhood years, when neither time nor circumstance had come between them, for that brief, happy summer's day. . . .

A speech, a regular attempt at a speech. It was not especially amusing, but it didn't go too badly either; the company drank, went on with dinner and resumed their conversation. Ditlef remarked dryly to his mother, "I never knew it was really me who wrote his books. Eh?"

But the lady of the house didn't laugh. She drank with her children and said, "Thank him, yes, thank him. It's very understandable, seeing how alone he was as a child. . . . Victoria, what are you doing?"

"I want to send the maid with this spray of lilac to thank him. Can't I do that?"

"No," said the Lieutenant.

After dinner the company dispersed to the different rooms, onto the large balcony and even into the garden. Johannes went down to the ground floor and entered a room facing the garden. There were people there already, a couple of smoking gentlemen, the landowner and another man, who were discussing their host's finances in an undertone. His property was neglected, overgrown, the fences down, the forests thinned out; it was rumored that he even had difficulty paying the surprisingly high insurance on the buildings and the furniture.

"How much is it all insured for?"

The landowner named the figure, a strikingly high one.

Come to that, they had never been sparing with money at the Castle; there the figures were always large ones. Consider, for example, the cost of a dinner like this! But now everything was said to be empty, even the lady's famous jewel case, and so the son-in-law's money was needed to restore their former splendor.

"How much is he worth, I wonder."

"Phew, there's no knowing how much."

Johannes got up and went out into the garden. The lilacs were in bloom, the scent of primula and narcissus, of jasmine and lily of the valley, wafted toward him. He found a corner by the wall and sat down on a stone, hidden from the world by shrubbery. He was exhausted by the emotional agitation, dead tired, his reason clouded; he thought of getting up and going home but kept sitting there, dull and listless. Then he hears a murmur of voices on the gravel path, someone is coming, he recognizes Victoria's voice. He holds his breath, and in another moment the Lieutenant's uniform also gleams through the foliage. The betrothed are taking a stroll together.

"It seems to me there's something wrong here," he says. "You listen to what he says, you sit there paying attention to his speech, and then you let out a yell. What did it really mean?"

She stops and stands tall before him. "Do you want to know?" she says.

"Yes."

She's silent.

"If it didn't mean anything, it doesn't matter," he goes on. "Then you don't have to tell me."

She eases up again. "It didn't mean anything," she says.

They resume their walk. The Lieutenant nervously twitches his epaulets and says loudly, "He'd better watch out. Otherwise an officer's hand might cuff his ears for him."

They took the path to the pavilion.

Johannes kept sitting on the stone for a while, dull and tormented as before. Everything was beginning to affect him with indifference. The Lieutenant had become suspicious of him, and his fiancée explained herself forthwith. She said what had to be said, assuaged the officer's heart and walked on with him. And the starlings were chattering in the branches above their heads. Well and good. God grant them a long life. . . . He had made a speech for her at dinner and torn his heart out; it had cost him dearly to correct and cover up her impertinent interruption, and she hadn't even thanked him. She had picked up her glass and taken a draft. Skoal! Look at me, see how prettily I drink. . . . By the way, you must watch a woman from the side when she drinks. Let her drink from a cup, a glass, anything whatever, but watch her from the side. She puts on such an act, it's simply awful. Pursing her lips, she dips only their outermost rim in the drink, and she gets desperate if you observe her hand as she does so. Altogether, don't look at a woman's hand. She can't stand it, she surrenders. She immediately starts pulling her hand back, posing it more and more exquisitely solely to hide a wrinkle, a crooked finger, or a less than perfectly shaped nail. Finally she can't bear it any longer and, quite beside herself, asks, What are you looking at? . . . One day she had kissed him, once upon a time, one summer. It was so long ago, God knows if it was even true. How was it, weren't they sitting on a bench? They talked together for a long time, and when they left he came so close to her that he touched her arm. Then, in front of an entrance, she kissed him. I love you! she said. . . . By now they had walked past, perhaps they were sitting in the pavilion. The Lieutenant would give him a smack on the ear, he said. He heard it quite clearly, he wasn't asleep; but he didn't get up and step forward either. An officer's hand, he said. Oh well, it didn't matter. . . .

He got up from the stone and followed them to the pavilion. It was empty. By the veranda of the main building Camilla was calling to him: coffee was being served in the garden room, so please! He went with her. There they sat, the engaged couple; there were also several others in the room. He got his coffee, withdrew, and found himself a seat.

Camilla began talking to him. Her complexion was so fair, her gaze so open; he couldn't resist her and joined in, answering her questions and laughing. Where had he been? In the garden? That wasn't true, she had looked in the garden and not found him. He had certainly not been in the garden.

"Victoria," she says, "was he in the garden?"

"I didn't see him," Victoria says.

The Lieutenant darts a furious glance at her, and to warn his fiancée he asks the landowner in a needlessly loud voice, "Did you say I could come and hunt woodcocks with you?"

"Certainly," the landowner answers, "you're welcome."

The Lieutenant looks at Victoria. She is silent and sits as before, doing nothing to stop him from going on this woodcock hunt at the landowner's. His face clouds over more and more, he strokes his mustache with nervous gestures.

Camilla asks Victoria another question.

At this moment the Lieutenant jumps up and says to the landowner, "Good, I'll come with you this evening, right away."

With that he leaves the room.

The landowner and a few others follow him.

A brief pause ensues.

Suddenly the door opens and the Lieutenant reenters. He's in a state of extreme agitation.

"Have you forgotten something?" Victoria asks, getting up.

He makes some hopping steps by the door, as if unable to stand still, and walks straight up to Johannes, whom he sort of jabs with his hand in passing. Then he runs back to the door and continues hopping about.

"Look out, man, you poked me in the eye," Johannes said, with a hollow laugh.

"You're mistaken," the Lieutenant replied. "I gave you a box on the ear. You understand? Understand?"

Johannes took out his handkerchief, wiped his eye and said, "You don't mean that. You must know I can fold you up and put you in my pocket."

Saying so, he stood up.

The Lieutenant hastened to open the door and left the room. "I mean it!" he screamed over his shoulder. "I mean it, you oaf!"

Then he closed the door with a bang.

Johannes sat down again.

Victoria had stopped in the middle of the room. She was gazing at him, white as a sheet.

"Did he punch you?" Camilla asked in utter amazement.

"By accident. He hit me in the eye. Would you like to have a look?"

"God, it's all red, there's blood. No, don't rub it, let me bathe it with some water. Your hanky is so coarse, here, take it back, I'll use my own. Who would believe it, straight in the eye!"

Victoria also held out her handkerchief. She didn't say anything. Then she walked slowly up to the glass door, where she remained with her back to the room, looking out. She was tearing her handkerchief into tiny shreds. A few minutes later she opened the door and left the garden room, quietly and without a word.

IX

Camilla came walking over to the mill, cheerful and straightforward. She was alone. She walked right into the small front room and said with a chuckle, "Pardon me for not knocking. There is such a roar from the river that I didn't think it would do any good." Looking around, she exclaimed, "Oh, what a delightful place! Just delightful! Where's Johannes? I know Johannes. How is his eye doing?"

She was offered a chair and sat down.

Johannes was sent for at the mill. His eye was inflamed and black and blue.

"I've come of my own accord," Camilla said as he approached. "I just felt like coming. You must continue to apply cold compresses to your eye."

"There's no need," he replied. "But bless you, what brings you here? Would you like to see the mill? Thank you for coming!" He put his arm around his mother, brought her forward and said, "This is my mother."

They went down to the mill. The old miller doffed his cap, made a deep bow and said something. Camilla couldn't hear him, but she smiled and said at random, "Thank you, thank you. Yes, I would very much like to see it."

The noise frightened her and she held Johannes' hand, glancing up at the two men with large, listening eyes in case they should say something. She looked just like a deaf person. The many wheels and contraptions in the mill filled her with wonder; she laughed, squeezed Johannes' hand in her eagerness, and pointed in every direction. The mill was stopped and started again so she could see how it worked.

Camilla kept speaking absurdly loud for quite a while after leaving the mill, as if the din were still echoing in her ears.

Johannes walked her back to the Castle.

"That he dared to poke you in the eye! Can you understand it? Then, of course, he slipped away immediately, going hunting with the landowner. It was a terribly unpleasant thing to have happened. Victoria didn't sleep all night, she told me."

"Then she can sleep tonight," he replied. "When do you think you'll be going home?"

"Tomorrow. When are you coming to town?"

"In the fall. May I see you this afternoon?"

"Certainly. Oh, how thrilling!" she cried. "You told me about a cave of yours, you have to show it to me."

"I'll come and get you," he said.

On his way home he sat for a long time on a rock, pondering. A warm, happy thought had occurred to him.

In the afternoon he went over to the Castle, stopped outside and asked for Camilla. While he was waiting, Victoria appeared at a second-floor window for a moment; she stared down at him, turned, and disappeared into the room.

Camilla came and he took her to the quarry and the cave. He was in an exceptionally peaceful and happy state of mind; the young girl diverted him, her cheerful, light-hearted words fluttered around him like small benedictions. Today the good spirits were hovering near. . . .

"Camilla, I recall your giving me a dagger once. It had a silver sheath. I put it away in a box with some other things because I had no use for it."

"So, you had no use for it, what then?"

"Well, you see, I've lost it."

"Oh, how unfortunate. But perhaps I can get you another one like it somewhere. I'll try."

They were on their way home.

"And do you remember that large medallion you gave me? It was quite thick, heavy with gold, and it came with a mount. Inside, the medallion had some kind words you'd written."

"Yes, I remember."

"Camilla, when I was abroad last year I gave the medallion away."

"Oh no, you did? Imagine, giving it away! Why?"

"I gave it to a young friend of mine, as a memento. He was a Russian. He fell on his knees and thanked me for it."

"Did it make him that happy? Goodness, he must've been fabulously happy, falling on his knees and all! I'll give you another medallion instead, to keep for yourself."

They had reached the road leading from the mill to the Castle.

Johannes stopped. "Something happened to me once near this thicket," he said. "I was taking a walk one evening, as I often did then, being very lonely, and it was summer with a clear sky. I lay down behind the thicket to think. Then two people came quietly walking along the road. The woman stopped. Her companion asked, 'Why are you stopping?' When he didn't get an answer, he asked again, 'Is something the matter?' 'No,' she replied, 'but you mustn't look at me like that.' 'I was simply looking at you,' he said. 'Yes,' she answers, 'I know perfectly well that you love me, but Papa won't allow it, you see; it's impossible.' 'Yes, I suppose it is,' he murmurs. Then she says,

'You're so broad there, on your hand; you have such unusually broad wrists!' And she closes her hand over his wrist."

Pause.

"Well, what happened?" Camilla asked.

"That I don't know," Johannes answered. "Why did she say that thing about his wrists?"

"Perhaps they looked nice. And then there was his white shirt right next to them—oh yes, I quite understand. Maybe she was in love with him too."

"Camilla!" he said. "If I was very much in love with you and waited a few years, I'm only asking . . . In a word, I'm not worthy of you, but do you think you could be mine some day, if I asked you next year, or two years from now?"

Pause.

Camilla, having suddenly turned crimson with confusion, twists her graceful figure back and forth and clasps her hands. He puts his arm around her and asks, "Do you think you could some day? Would you?"

"Yes," she answers, letting her body fall against his.

The following day he walks her to the pier. He kisses her small hands with their childlike, innocent expression and is filled with gratitude and joy.

Victoria hadn't come along.

"Why didn't anyone come with you?"

With terror in her eyes, Camilla relates that the Castle was plunged in the most dreadful grief. A telegram had arrived that morning, the master had turned white as a sheet, the old chamberlain and his wife had cried out in pain—Otto had been shot and killed on the hunt yesterday evening.

Johannes clutched Camilla's arm. "Dead? The Lieutenant?"

"Yes. They are on the way here with the body. It's awful."

They walked on, absorbed in their own thoughts; they were brought back to reality only by the people on the pier, the ship, and the shouts of command. Shyly, Camilla gave him her hand, which he kissed, saying, "Well, Camilla, I'm not worthy of you, not in the least. But I'll do my best to make you happy, if you will be mine."

"I want to be yours. I've wanted it all along, all along."

"I'll be coming in a few days," he said. "In a week I'll see you again."

She was on board. He waved to her, keeping it up until he could no longer make her out. When he turned to go home, Victoria was standing behind him; she too was holding up her handkerchief and waving good-bye to Camilla.

"I was a bit late," she said.

He didn't answer. What could he say? Console her for her loss, congratulate her, press her hand? Her voice was so toneless and her face so distraught, bearing the marks of a wrenching experience.

People were leaving the pier.

"Your eye is still red," she said, starting to walk away. She looked back over her shoulder.

He hadn't moved.

Then she quickly turned around and went up to him.

"Otto is dead," she said harshly, her eyes blazing. "You don't say a word, you're so superior. He was a hundred thousand times better than you, do you hear? Do you know how he died? He was shot, his whole head was blown to pieces, his whole stupid little head. He was a hundred thousand . . ."

Bursting into sobs, she started on her way with long, despairing steps.

Late that evening there is a knock at the miller's; Johannes opens the door and looks out: Victoria is standing outside, beckoning to him. He follows her. She clutches his hand and leads him up to the road; her hand is cold as ice.

"You'd better sit down," he said. "Sit down and rest awhile; you are all nerves."

They sit down.

"What must you think of me, not being able to leave you alone for a moment!" she murmurs.

"You're very unhappy," he says. "Now, Victoria, listen to me and compose yourself. Can I help you with anything?"

"For heaven's sake, you must forgive me for what I said this morning!" she begs him. "Yes, I'm very unhappy, I've been unhappy for years. I said he was a hundred thousand times better than you; it wasn't true, forgive me! He's dead, and he was my fiancé, that's all. Do you imagine it was of my own free will? Johannes, do you see this? It's my engagement ring, I got it a long time ago, a long, long time ago; now I'm throwing it away—throwing it away!" And she throws the ring into the woods; they both hear it fall. "It was Papa who wanted it. Papa is poor, he's an absolute beggar, and Otto would come into so much money one day. 'You must do it,' Papa told me. 'I won't,' I replied. 'Think of your parents,' he said, 'think of the Castle, our ancient name, my honor.' 'All right, then I'll do it,' I replied. 'Wait three years and I'll do it.' Papa thanked me and waited, Otto waited, they all waited; but I got the ring right away. Then a long time passed, and I came to realize it was no use. 'Why wait any longer? Bring me my husband,' I told Papa. 'God bless you,' he said, thanking me again for what I was about to do. And Otto came. I didn't go to meet him on the pier, I stood at my window and saw him drive up. Then I rushed to Mama's room and went down on my knees before her. 'What's wrong, my child?' she asks. 'I can't,' I reply, 'I can't take him; he's here, he's standing downstairs. I'd rather we insure my life and I'll be lost in the bay or the waterfall, that's better for me.' Mama turns deathly pale and weeps over me. Papa comes in. 'Now then, Victoria, my dear,' he says, 'it's time you come down and welcome him.' 'I can't, I can't,' I answer and repeat what I'd said, that he should have mercy on me and insure my life. Papa doesn't utter a word but sits down all in a tremor, trying to think. When I see that I say, 'Bring me my husband, I'll take him.' "

Victoria pauses. She's shaking. Johannes takes her other hand too and warms it.

"Thank you," she says. "Johannes, please hold my hand tight! Please! God, how warm you are! I'm so grateful to you. But you must forgive me for what I said on the pier."

"Oh, that was forgotten long ago. Would you like me to get you a shawl?"

"No, thanks. But I can't understand why I'm shivering when my head is so hot. Johannes, I ought to ask your forgiveness for so many things—"

"No, no, don't. There, now you're calmer. Sit still."

"You spoke, you gave a speech for me. I didn't know what I

was doing from the moment you got up until you sat down again; I only heard your voice. It was like an organ, and the fact that it charmed me so made me desperate. Papa asked me why I'd screamed and interrupted you; he felt very bad about it. But Mama didn't ask, she understood. I'd told Mama everything, I told her years ago, and I repeated it two years ago when I returned from the city. That was the time I met you."

"Let's not talk about it."

"No, but forgive me, do you hear, be merciful! What in the world am I to do? There's Papa at home, pacing up and down in his office; it's so awful for him. Tomorrow is Sunday; he has decided to let the servants have the day off, that's the only decision he has made today. His face is gray and he doesn't speak, that's how his son-in-law's death affects him. I told Mama I was going to you. 'You and I must both go to the city with the chamberlain and his wife tomorrow,' she said. 'I'm going to Johannes,' I repeated. 'Papa can't find money for all three of us, he's staying on here,' she said; then she went on talking about other things. I walked to the door. Mama looked at me. 'I'm going to him now,' I said for the last time. Mama followed me to the door, kissed me and said, 'God bless you both, then!'"

Johannes let go of her hands and said, "There, you're warm now."

"Thanks so much, yes, now I'm quite warm. . . . 'God bless you both,' she said. I told Mama everything, she has known all along. 'But darling, whom then do you love, my child?' she asked. 'You can still ask about that?' I said. 'Johannes is the one I love, he's the only one I've loved all my life, loved, loved. . . .'"

He made a movement. "It's late. Don't you think they'll start worrying about you at home?"

"No," she said. "You know it's you I love, Johannes; you must have seen that? I've longed for you so terribly during these years, more than anybody would ever understand. I've walked along this road and thought, Now I'll keep to the woods near the road, that's where *he* preferred to walk. And that's what I do. The day I heard you'd come home I put on a light dress, light yellow; I was sick with suspense and longing and kept walking in and out of every door. 'How radiant you look today!' Mama said. I was saying to myself all the time, 'He has

come home again! He's gorgeous and he's back—that's him!'
The next day I couldn't stand it any longer, so I put on my light
dress again and went up to the quarry to meet you. Do you remember? And I did meet you, but I didn't pick flowers, as I
said, that was not what I came for. You were no longer glad to
see me again, but thanks anyway for the chance to meet you. I
hadn't seen you for over two years. You had a twig in your
hand and were swishing it in the air when I came; after you left
I picked up the twig, hid it, and took it home with me—"

"Yes, but Victoria," he said in a trembling voice, "you mustn't
say such things to me anymore."

"No," she replied anxiously and seized his hand. "No, I
mustn't. I can see you don't like me to." She began patting his
hand nervously. "No, I can't really expect you to. And besides,
I've hurt you ever so much. Don't you think you'll be able to
forgive me sometime?"

"Oh yes, everything. It's not that."

"What is it then?"

Pause.

"I'm engaged," he said.

X

The following day—a Sunday—the Castle proprietor came to
the miller in person and asked him to show up around noon
and drive Lieutenant Otto's body to the steamer. The miller
didn't understand and stared at him, but the proprietor explained briefly that all his hired people had been given the day
off; they had gone to church, none of the servants were home.

The proprietor had apparently not slept the night before, he
looked cadaverous and, what's more, was unshaven. Yet, he
swung his cane in his usual way and held himself erect.

The miller put on his best coat and was off. When he had
hitched up the horses, the master himself helped him carry the
body out to the carriage. It was all done quietly, almost secre-
tively; no observer was present.

The miller drove off to the pier. He was followed by the
chamberlain and his wife, in addition to the lady of the house

and Victoria. They were all on foot. The master could be seen standing alone on the steps, waving repeated good-byes; the wind ruffled his gray hair.

When the body had been brought on board, the mourners followed. From the ship's rail, the mistress called to the miller on shore, asking him to say good-bye to the master for them, and Victoria asked him the same.

The ship steamed off. The miller followed it with his eyes for a long while. There was a strong wind and the bay was rough; it was a quarter of an hour before the ship disappeared behind the islands. The miller drove home.

He stabled the horses, fed them, and was about to go in and bring the master the ladies' good wishes. However, the back entrance happened to be locked. He walked round the house and tried to get in by the main entrance; the front door was locked too. It's the dinner hour and the master is taking a nap, he thought. But being a punctilious man who liked to fulfill his promises, he went down to the servants' hall looking for someone to whom he could deliver the message. There wasn't a soul around. He went out again, searched all over, even strayed into the maids' room. There was no one there either. The whole place was deserted.

He was just about to leave when he noticed a gleam of light in the Castle basement. He stopped short. Through the small barred windows he could clearly see a man entering the basement with a lighted candle in one hand and a silk-upholstered red chair in the other. It was the master. He had shaved and was wearing evening dress, as if for a celebration. Maybe I could knock on the window and pass on his wife's good wishes that way, the miller thought, but he remained where he was.

The master looked around, shone the light about him and looked around. He pulled out a sack which seemed to contain hay or grain stalks and put it by the entrance. Then he poured some liquid over the sack from a can. Next, he brought some crates, straw, and a discarded flower-stand up to the door and sprayed it all from the can. The miller noticed that he took great pains not to dirty his fingers or his clothes while doing this. He took the candle stub, placed it on top of the sack, and carefully packed straw around it. Then he sat down in the chair.

His eyes glued to the basement window, the miller grew more and more thunderstruck as he stared at these preparations, and a dark suspicion entered his soul. The master sat quite still in his chair, watching the candle burn lower and lower; he kept his hands folded. The miller sees him flick a speck of dust from the black sleeve of his tailcoat and fold his hands again.

Then the horrified old miller lets out a scream.

The master turns his head and looks out the window. Suddenly he leaps to his feet and comes to the window, where he stops to stare outside. His eyes mirror all the world's suffering. His mouth oddly twisted, he reaches toward the window with a pair of clenched fists, threateningly, without a word; in the end he threatens with only one hand and backs away across the basement floor. When he bumps into the chair, the candle tips over. Instantly a huge flame leaps up.

The miller screams and takes flight. For a moment he rushes about the yard frantic with terror and at his wits' end. He runs up to the basement window, kicks the panes to pieces and cries out; then he bends down, grips the iron bars with his fists and tugs at them, bending them and ripping them out.

At that point he hears a voice coming from the basement, a voice without words, a groan, as if from a dead man underground; when he hears it again, the horror-struck miller flees from the window, across the yard, down the road and home. He didn't dare look back.

When he arrived on the scene with Johannes a few minutes later, the entire Castle, that grand old wooden house, was a sea of flames. A couple of men from the pier had also come, but they were equally unable to do anything. All was lost.

But the miller's lips were silent as the grave.

XI

Asked what love is, some will say it is nothing but a wind whispering among the roses and then dying down. But often it is like an unbreakable seal that holds for a lifetime, until death. God created it of many different kinds and has seen it endure or perish:

Two mothers walk along the road talking together. One is dressed in cheerful blue because her lover has just returned from a journey. The other is in mourning. She had three daughters, two dark, the third one blond, and the blond one died. It's been ten years since, ten whole years, and still the mother wears mourning for her.

"What a glorious day!" exclaims the mother in blue, rejoicing and clapping her hands. "I'm drunk with the warmth, I'm drunk with love, I'm filled with happiness. I could strip myself naked right here, on the road, stretch out my arms to the sun and blow it a kiss."

But the woman in black is silent and neither smiles nor answers.

"Are you still mourning your little girl?" asks the one in blue in the innocence of her heart. "Hasn't it been ten years since she died?"

"Yes," the one in black replies. "She would've been fifteen now."

To console her, the one in blue says, "But you have other daughters, alive, you still have two left."

"Yes," the one in black sobs, "but neither of them is blond. She who died was so blond."

And the two mothers part and go their separate ways, each with her love. . . .

But these same two dark daughters also had each their love, and they loved the same man.

He came to the elder one and said, "I would like to ask your advice, because I love your sister. Yesterday I was unfaithful to her, she surprised me kissing your maid in the hallway; she gave a little cry, a mere whimper, and passed on. What shall I do now? I love your sister, speak to her for heaven's sake and help me!"

The elder sister turned pale and clutched at her heart; but she smiled as if about to bless him and answered, "I'll help you."

The next day he went to the younger sister, threw himself on his knees before her and confessed his love.

She gave him the once-over and said, "I'm afraid I cannot spare more than a ten-krone note, if that's what you mean. But go to my sister, she has more."

And with that she left him, tossing her head.

But when she reached her room she threw herself on the floor and wrung her hands for love.

It's winter and cold outside, with fog, dust and wind. Johannes is back in town, in his old room, where he can hear the poplars creak against the woodwork and has greeted the dawn from the window more than once. Now the sun is gone.

His thoughts had all along been diverted by his work, those large sheets that he covered with writing, of which there were more and more as the winter wore on. It was a series of fairy tales from the land of his fantasy, an endless night with a red sun suffusing the sky.

But his days varied, the good alternating with the bad, and sometimes when he was working at his best a thought, a pair of eyes, a word from the past would strike him and suddenly break his mood. Then he would get up from his chair and start walking up and down in his room, from wall to wall; he had done this so often that a white track had been worn in the floor, and the track grew whiter every day. . . .

Today, being unable to work, unable to think, unable to shake off my memories, I begin to write down what happened to me one night. Dear reader, today is one of those terribly difficult days for me. It's snowing outside, the street is almost deserted, everything is sad, and my soul feels utterly desolate. I have spent hours trying to collect myself a little, walking the streets and afterward pacing up and down in my room, but it's already afternoon and things are no better. I ought to be warm, but I'm cold and pale as a dying day. Dear reader, in this state I'll try to write about a thrilling white night. Work will force me to be calm, and in a few hours I may be cheerful again. . . .

There is a knock on the door and Camilla Seier, his young, secret fiancée, comes in. He puts down his pen and gets up. They smile and say hello.

"You haven't asked me about the ball," she says at once, throwing herself into a chair. "I danced every single dance. It went on till three o'clock in the morning. I danced with Richmond."

"Thanks so much for coming, Camilla. I feel so wretchedly

low and you're so cheerful; that will help, don't you think? And what did you wear at the ball?"

"Red, naturally. My goodness, I can't recall, but I must have talked and laughed a lot. It was simply enchanting. Yes, I wore red, no sleeves, not a bit. Richmond is at the London legation."

"I see."

"His parents are English, but he was born here. What have you done to your eyes? They're all red. Have you been crying?"

"No," he answers, laughing, "but I've been staring into my fairy tales, where the sun is very strong. Camilla, please try not to tear up that sheet of paper any more than you already have, that's a good girl!"

"Good heavens, how thoughtless of me. Sorry, Johannes."

"It doesn't really matter, it's only some notes. But tell me, you had a rose in your hair, didn't you?"

"Oh yes. A red rose; it was almost black. Do you know something, Johannes? We could go to London on our honeymoon. It's not nearly as dreadful as people say, and the fog and all is just a pack of lies."

"Who told you?"

"Richmond. He said so last night, and he knows all about it. You know Richmond, don't you?"

"No, I don't. He proposed my health once; he had diamond studs in his shirtfront. That's all I remember about him."

"He's absolutely delicious. Just imagine, he came up to me, bowed and said, 'My young lady, perhaps you don't remember me. . . .' Ooh, I gave him the rose."

"You did? What rose?"

"The one I had in my hair. I gave it to him."

"You're very much taken with Richmond, I believe?"

Blushing, she puts up a spirited defense. "Certainly not, not a bit. You can easily like someone, think well of someone, without . . . Shame on you, Johannes, you must be mad! I'll never mention his name again."

"God bless you, Camilla, I didn't mean—you really mustn't think . . . On the contrary, I'm going to thank him for entertaining you."

"Yes, be sure to do that—just you dare! I, for one, won't say another word to him, ever."

Pause.

"Well, let's leave it at that," he says. "Are you going already?"

"Yes, I can't stay any longer. How far have you got with your work by now? Mama was asking about it. Imagine, I hadn't seen Victoria for weeks and just now I ran across her."

"Just now?"

"On my way here. She smiled. But goodness, how faded she looked! Listen, won't you come visiting soon?"

"Yes, soon," he answers, jumping up. His face has turned all red. "Maybe in the next few days. I must write something first, I have an idea, a conclusion to my fairy tales. Oh, I am going to write something, all right, I certainly am! Imagine the earth seen from above, like a beautiful, fantastic papal gown. In its folds you see people walking about, in pairs; it's a quiet evening, the hour of love. I'm calling it 'The Spirit of Life.' I think it will be grand; I've had this vision so often, and every time it feels as though my breast were going to burst and I could embrace the whole earth. There are people and animals and birds and, Camilla, they are all having their hour of love. A wave of rapture awaits them, their eyes grow more ardent, their breath quickens. Then a delicate blush rises from the earth, a blush of bashfulness from all those naked hearts, and the night takes on a rose-red hue. But far away, in the background, sit the big sleeping mountains; they have seen and heard nothing. And in the morning God casts his warm sun over everything. 'The Spirit of Life,' I'm calling it."

"I see."

"Yes. And when I've finished it I'll come. Thanks so much for dropping by, Camilla. And forget what I said. I meant no harm."

"I've forgotten it already. And I won't ever mention his name again. I won't, not ever."

Next morning Camilla drops by again. She is pale and unusually restless.

"What's the matter?" he asks.

"With me? Nothing," she shoots back. "You're the one I love. You really mustn't think there's anything the matter with me and that I don't love you. No, I'll tell you what I've been thinking: we won't go to London. What would we do there? The man obviously didn't know what he was talking about, there's more fog there than he thinks. You're looking at me, why? I didn't mention his name. What a liar! He told me a pack of lies. We won't go to London."

He looks at her, catching on. "No, we won't go to London," he says thoughtfully.

"Right. So we won't do that. Have you written that piece about the spirit of life? Gee, I think it's so interesting. Johannes, you have to finish it real soon and come see us. The hour of love, wasn't that it? And a ravishing papal gown with folds and a rose-red night—gee, how well I still remember what you told me about it! I haven't been to see you very often lately, but from now on I'll come every day and see if you're finished."

"I'll finish it very soon," he says, continuing to look at her.

"Today I took your books and put them in my own room. I'm going to reread them; it won't be the least tiring, I'm looking forward to it. Look, Johannes, why won't you, please, walk me home? I'm not sure it's quite safe for me all the way home. No, I'm not sure. There may be someone waiting for me outside, yes, someone who sticks around waiting for me. I almost think so. . . ." Suddenly she bursts into tears and stammers, "I called him a liar, I wish I hadn't. I feel very sorry about that. He didn't lie to me; on the contrary, he was always . . . We're going to have some visitors on Tuesday; he won't be coming, though, but listen, *you* must come. Promise? Still, I shouldn't have said those nasty things about him. I'm wondering what you think of me. . . ."

"I'm beginning to understand you," he said.

She flings her arms around his neck and hides her face on his breast, trembling and distraught.

"But I love you too," she exclaims. "You mustn't think I don't. I do not love him alone, it's not as bad as all that. When you asked me last year I was so glad, but then he came along. I can't figure it out. Johannes, is it so very terrible of me? Perhaps I love him a tiny bit more than you, I can't help that, it just came over me. Good gracious, I haven't slept for nights since I saw him, and I love him more and more. What shall I do? You're so much older, you must tell me. He came here with me, he's standing out there waiting to see me home, and he may feel cold by now. Johannes, do you despise me? I haven't kissed him, no, that I haven't, you must believe me; I just gave him my rose. Why don't you answer me, Johannes? You must tell me what to do, because I can't stand it any longer."

Johannes sat quite still listening to her. "There is nothing I can tell you," he said.

"Thank you, thank you, Johannes, dear; it's so sweet of you not to be furious with me," she said, wiping away her tears. "But you mustn't think I don't love you too. By God, I'll come and see you much more often than before and do everything you desire. It's just that I love him more. I didn't want it that way. It's not my fault."

He got up without a word; having put on his hat, he said, "Shall we go?"

They walked down the stairs.

Richmond was standing outside. He was a dark-haired young man with brown eyes sparkling with youth and life. The frost had made him rosy-cheeked.

"Are you cold?" said Camilla, flying to him.

Her voice quavered with emotion. Suddenly she darted back to Johannes, slipped her arm into his and said, "Forgive me for not asking you too if you were cold. You didn't put on your overcoat; shall I go and get it? No? Then button up your jacket at least."

She buttoned his jacket.

Johannes gave Richmond his hand. He was in a curiously absent state of mind, as if what was happening didn't really concern him. He smiled uncertainly, a kind of half smile, and murmured, "Glad to see you again."

Richmond gave no sign of either guilt or dissimulation. When he shook hands with Johannes, his face lighted up with the joy of recognition and he made a very deep bow.

"I recently saw one of your books in a bookseller's window in London," he said. "It had been translated. It was so nice seeing it there, a greeting from home."

Camilla walked in the middle, looking up at them by turns. Finally she said, "So you'll be coming on Tuesday, then, Johannes," adding with a laugh, "sorry to be thinking only of my own things." But the next moment she turned remorsefully to

Richmond and asked him to come as well. They were all people both of them knew. Victoria and her mother were also invited, together with some dozen others, no more.

Suddenly Johannes stopped and said, "You know, I think I may as well turn back."

"See you Tuesday," Camilla replied.

Richmond grasped his hand and pressed it cordially.

And the two young people went on their way, alone and happy.

XII

The mother in blue was in the most terrible suspense; she expected a signal from the garden any moment and the path was not clear: nobody could pass through as long as her husband refused to leave. Ugh, that husband, that forty-year-old balding husband! What horrible thought could have made him turn so pale this evening, causing him to sit there in his chair, immovable, unrelenting, staring at his newspaper?

She didn't have a moment's peace; it was eleven o'clock already. She had put the children to bed long ago, but her husband didn't leave. What if the signal sounded, the door was opened with that darling little key—what if the two men met, face to face, and looked one another in the eye! She didn't dare complete the thought.

She went into the darkest corner of the room, wrung her hands, and at last said straight out, "It's eleven o'clock. If you really mean to go to the club, you must leave now."

He got up at once, even paler than before, and went out of the room, out of the house.

Once outside the garden, he stops and listens to a whistle, a little signal. Steps are heard on the gravel, a key is inserted in the lock and turned, and a moment later two shadows appear on the living-room curtain.

He recognized the signal, the steps, and the two shadows on the curtain; it was all familiar to him.

He goes to the club. It's open, there is light in the windows; but he doesn't go in. He wanders about the streets and in front of his garden for two quarters of an hour, for two endless quarters of an hour. Let me wait another quarter of an hour, he thinks, and he extends it to three. Then he enters the garden, mounts the steps, and rings at his own front door.

The maid answers the bell, barely sticking her head out the door, and says, "The mistress has long since—"

She stops, seeing who it is.

"To be sure, gone to bed," he replies. "Will you go tell your mistress that her husband has come home."

The maid goes. She knocks at her mistress's room and gives the message through the closed door: "I was to tell you that the master has come back."

From inside the mistress asks, "What are you saying, my husband has come back? Who asked you to tell me this?"

"The master himself. He's standing outside."

A confused lament is heard from the mistress's room; there are breathless whispers, a door is opened and closed. Then all's quiet.

The master comes in. His wife meets him with death in her heart.

"The club was closed," he says quickly, out of sheer pity. "I sent word so as not to alarm you."

She collapses in a chair, comforted, delivered, saved. In this blissful mood, her kind heart overflows and she asks after her husband's health. "You are so pale. Is something the matter with you, my dear?"

"I'm not cold," he replies.

"But has anything happened to you? Your face is so strangely distorted."

"No, I'm smiling," the husband says. "It's my way of smiling. I want this grimace to be uniquely my own."

She listens to these brief, hoarse words and doesn't understand, she can't figure them out at all. What does he mean to say?

Suddenly he clasps her in an iron embrace, hugging her with dreadful force as he whispers close to her face, "What do you say to putting horns on him—on the one who just left—putting horns on him?"

She gives a scream and summons the maid. He lets go of her with a dry, noiseless laugh, opening his mouth wide and slapping his thighs.

In the morning the wife's kind heart wins out again and she says to her husband, "You had a strange attack last night; it's over now, but you still look pale."

"Yes," he answers, "it's a strain being witty at my age. I won't ever try again."

After discussing many kinds of love, Munken Vendt tells about yet another kind, beginning, This is how intoxicating a certain kind of love can be!

A young couple have just come home, their long honeymoon is over and they settle down.

A shooting star streaked across the sky above their roof.

In the summer the couple went for walks together, never leaving each other's side. They picked red and yellow and blue flowers which they gave one another; they watched the grass swaying in the breeze and heard the birds singing in the woods, and every word they spoke was like a caress. In the winter they drove with harness bells on their horses, the sky was blue, and high above them the stars zoomed along on the eternal plains.

Many, many years went by in this manner. The young couple had three children, and their hearts were as loving as on the first day, exchanging their first kiss.

Then the proud gentleman is stricken with an illness, an illness that chained him to his bed for ever so long and sorely tried his wife's patience. The day he was well enough to rise from his bed he didn't recognize himself; the illness had disfigured him and robbed him of his hair.

He suffered and brooded. Then one morning he said, "Now you won't love me anymore, I suppose?"

But his wife blushed, threw her arms around him and kissed him as ardently as in the spring of their youth and said, "I—I'll love you, love you forever. I shall never forget it was me and no one else you chose and made so happy."

And she went into her room and cut off her golden hair, so she would be like the husband she loved.

Again many, many years went by; the young couple were getting on in years and their children were grown up. They shared every happiness as before; in the summer they still walked in the fields and saw the grass waving, and in the winter they bundled up in their furs and went for rides under a starry sky. And their hearts continued to be warm and glad, as though cheered by some wonderful wine.

Then the wife became paralyzed. Unable to use her legs, the old lady had to be in a wheelchair, which the husband himself moved about. Her misfortune brought unspeakable suffering, and sorrow dug deep furrows in her face.

One day she said, "Now I would like to die. I'm so paralyzed and so ugly, and your face is so beautiful; you cannot kiss me anymore or love me as before."

But the husband embraces her, flushed with emotion, and says, "I—I love you more, more than my life, dearest one; I love you as on the first day, that first moment when you gave me the rose. You remember? You offered me the rose and looked at me with your beautiful eyes; the rose had the same scent as you, you blushed like a rose, and all my senses were intoxicated. But now I love you even more, you're more beautiful than in your youth, and my heart thanks you and blesses you for each day you have been mine."

The husband goes to his room, pours acid on his face to disfigure it and says to his wife, "I was unlucky enough to get some acid on my face, my cheeks are full of burns, and I'm afraid you won't love me anymore."

"Oh, my bridegroom, my beloved!" the old woman stammers, kissing his hands. "You're more beautiful than any man on earth, even today your voice sets my heart ablaze, and I love you unto death."

XIII

Johannes runs across Camilla in the street; she is with her mother, her father, and young Richmond. They stop their carriage and chat amiably with him.

Camilla seizes him by the arm and says, "You didn't come! You can't imagine what a great party we had; we waited for you till the last, but you didn't come."

"I couldn't make it," he said.

"Sorry I haven't been up to see you since," she went on. "I'll be sure to come one of these days, after Richmond leaves. Oh, what a party we had! Victoria became ill and was taken home, did you hear? I'll go see her soon. I dare say she's much better now, perhaps quite well again. I've given Richmond a medallion nearly identical to yours. Listen, Johannes, you must promise me to look after your stove; when you're writing you forget about everything and your room gets ice-cold. Then you must ring for the maid."

"All right, I'll ring for the maid," he replied.

Mrs. Seier also talked to him, inquiring about his work, that piece about the spirit of life; how was it going? She was eagerly awaiting his next project.

Johannes gave the necessary answers, made a deep bow and watched the carriage drive off. How little it all concerned him, this carriage, these people, this chatter! A cold, empty feeling invaded him; it stayed with him all the way home. In the street near his entrance a man was strolling up and down, an old acquaintance, the former tutor at the Castle.

Johannes nodded to him.

He was dressed in a long warm coat that had been carefully brushed, and there was a brisk and determined air about him.

"You see before you your friend and colleague," he said. "Give me your hand, young man. God has led me in wondrous ways since we met; I'm married, I have a home, a little garden, a wife. Miracles still happen. Do you have any comment on my last observation?"

Johannes looks at him in astonishment.

"That is, approved. Well, you see, I was tutoring her son. She has a son, offspring from her first marriage; she'd been married before, of course, she was a widow. Yes, I married a widow. You may object that this could not have been in the cards for me, but there it is: I married a widow. The child was there from the beginning. You see, I go around looking at the garden and the widow, thinking long and hard about the matter. Suddenly I have it, and I say to myself, 'Oh well, it may not have been in the cards, and so on, but I'll do it anyway, I'll go for it; as likely as not, it's written in the stars.' So there, that's how it happened."

"Congratulations!" Johannes said.

"Stop! Not another word! I know what you're going to say.

And what about her, the first one, you will say, have you forgotten the eternal love of your youth? That's exactly what you
will say. May I then, on my part, ask you, sir, where my first and
only eternal love ended up? Didn't she take a captain of artillery? And besides, let me pose another little question to you:
Have you ever, ever seen a man getting the one he was supposed
to have? I haven't. There is a legend about someone whose
prayers God answered in this respect, he won his first and only
love. But it didn't bring him much joy. Why not? you'll ask
again, and I answer you thus: for the simple reason that she died
immediately afterward—immediately afterward, do you hear,
ha-ha, the very next moment. That's the way things are. Naturally you don't get the woman you should have; but if by some
damn fluke of fair play it ever does happen, she dies immediately afterward. There's always a catch somewhere. And so a
man has no choice but to find himself another love, of the best
possible quality, and he doesn't have to die of the change. Take
it from me, things are so wisely arranged by nature that he bears
up extremely well. Just look at me."

"I can see you're doing very well," Johannes said.

"Exceedingly well, so far. Listen, feel, and see! Have I
foundered in a sea of cheerless sorrows? I have clothes, shoes, a
house and home, a spouse, children—well, the boy, you know.
But what I was going to say was this: with regard to my poetry,
I'll answer you on the spot. My dear young colleague, I'm older
than you and perhaps a trifle better endowed by nature. I keep
my poetic writings in my drawer. They are to be published after my death. But then you won't derive any pleasure from
them, you will remonstrate. There you're wrong again; mean-
while, you see, I'm delighting my family with them. In the evening, when the lamp is lighted, I unlock the drawer, take out
my poems and read them aloud to my wife and the boy. One is
forty, the other twelve, and both are enchanted. If you drop by
sometime, you'll get supper and a hot toddy. That is an invitation. May God preserve you from death."

He gave Johannes his hand. Suddenly he asked, "Have you
heard about Victoria?"

"About Victoria? No. Or rather, I heard just now, a moment
ago—"

"Haven't you seen her ailing, getting more and more gray under the eyes?"

"I haven't seen her since I was home in the spring. Is she still sick?"

The tutor gave a comically harsh answer, stamping his foot: "Yes."

"I just heard . . . No, I certainly haven't seen her ailing, I never happened to meet her. Is she very ill?"

"Very. Probably dead by now. You understand?"

Perplexed, Johannes looked at the man, at his door, wondering whether to go in or stay, then back at the man, at his long coat and his hat; he gave a pained, bewildered smile, as if in distress.

The old tutor continued with a menacing air: "Another example, can you deny it? She didn't get the one she should have had either, her childhood sweetheart, a gorgeous young lieutenant. He went hunting one evening, a shot hits him between the eyes and splits his head in two. There he lay, a victim of that little catch which God had prepared for him. Victoria, his bride, starts ailing, a worm was gnawing at her, riddling her heart like a sieve; we, her friends, could see it happening. Then a few days ago she went to a party at the home of some family called Seier; she told me, by the way, that you were also supposed to be there but didn't come. To make a long story short, at this party she overtaxes her strength; memories of her beloved crowd in upon her and make her kick up her heels out of sheer bravado—she dances and dances all evening, dances like mad. Then she takes a tumble and the floor turns red underneath her; they lift her up, carry her out and drive her home. She didn't last for very long."

The tutor walks right up to Johannes and says harshly, "Victoria is dead."

Johannes gropes with his hands like a blind man, as if trying to ward off a blow. "Dead? When did she die? Did you say Victoria is dead?"

"She's dead," the tutor answers. "She died this morning, well, this forenoon." He put his hand in his pocket and pulled out a thick letter. "She entrusted me with this letter for you. Here it is. 'After my death,' she said. She's dead. I've delivered the letter. My mission is accomplished."

And without saying good-bye, without another word, the tutor turned on his heel and strolled slowly down the street and disappeared.

Johannes stood there with the letter in his hand. Victoria was dead. He spoke her name aloud again and again, in an emotionless, almost callous voice. He looked down at the letter and recognized the handwriting; there were capital letters and small letters, the lines were straight, and she who had written them was dead!

He makes his way through the door and up the stairs, finds the right key and lets himself in. His room is cold and dark. He sits down by the window and, by the last remainder of daylight, reads Victoria's letter. She wrote:

Dear Johannes!

When you read this letter I'll be dead! Everything seems so strange to me now, I no longer feel ashamed before you and write to you as if there were no reasons not to. Before, when I was still fully alive, I would rather have suffered night and day than write to you again, but now I have begun to die and I don't think like that any longer. Strangers have seen me bleed, the doctor has examined me and seen that I've only got part of one lung left, so why should I feel embarrassed about anything?

I've been lying here in bed thinking about the last words I spoke to you. It was that evening in the woods. It didn't occur to me then that they were to be my last words, or I would have said good-bye to you then and there and thanked you. Now I won't see you anymore, so I'm sorry I didn't throw myself at your feet and kiss your shoes and the ground you walked on, to show you how much I loved you, more than words can express. I've been lying here yesterday and today wishing I was well enough to go home again, to walk in the woods and find the place where we sat when you held my hands, because then I could lie down there and see if I couldn't find some traces of you and kiss all the heather nearby. But now I can't go home, unless I should get a little better perhaps, as Mama thinks.

Dear Johannes! When I think about it, how odd it seems that all I've managed to do is to come into the world and love you and now say good-bye to life. I cannot tell you how strange it feels to lie here and wait for the day and the hour. Step by step, I'm withdrawing from the bustle in the street, with its people and its clatter of carriages; I doubt I'll ever see the spring again, and these houses and streets and the trees in the park will still be here when I'm gone. Today I managed to sit up in bed and look out the window for a while. Down by the corner two people met, bowed to each other and shook hands, and laughed at what they said; but then it seemed so strange to me that I who lay watching it all was going to die. And I thought: those two down there don't know that I'm lying here awaiting my time, but even if they did they would probably say hello and chat just like now. Yesterday evening, when it was dark, I thought my last hour had come; my heart was starting to skip beats, and it was as though I could already hear eternity rushing toward me in the distance. But the next moment I returned from afar and began breathing again. It was an absolutely indescribable feeling. But Mama thinks that I was probably just remembering the sound of the river and the waterfall at home.

Good God, if you only knew how I have loved you, Johannes! I haven't had a chance to show you, so much has stood in the way, above all my own nature. Papa was hard on himself the same way, and I am his daughter. But now that I am to die and it is all too late, I write to you once again to let you know. I ask myself why I'm doing it, since it can't be of any interest to you, especially since I won't even be alive anymore; but I would like to be close to you till the end, so as not to feel more abandoned than ever. When you read this, it will be as though I can see your shoulders and your hands, and every movement you make as you hold the letter in front of you while reading it. That way we aren't so far away from each other, I say to myself. I cannot send for you, I haven't the right to. Mama wanted to send for you already two days ago, but I preferred to write. Also, I'd rather you remember me as I used to be, before I became ill. I remember that you . . . (here some words are missing) . . . my eyes and eyebrows; but they aren't the same either anymore. That is another reason I didn't want you to come. And I also want to ask you not to view me in the coffin. True, I'll look about the same as when I was alive, only somewhat paler, and I'll be in a yellow dress, but you would still be sorry if you came and saw me.

I've been writing this letter off and on all day, and still I haven't been able to tell you one thousandth of what I wanted to say. It's so terrible for me to die, I don't want to; I'm still hoping to God I might get a little better, even if only until the spring. Then the days are light and there are leaves on the trees. If I got well again, I would never be mean to you anymore, Johannes. How I've wept thinking about it! Oh, I would go out and stroke every cobblestone and stop and thank every step on the stairs I passed, and be kind to everybody. It wouldn't matter how much I suffered as long as I was allowed to live. I would never again complain about anything, no, I would smile at anyone who attacked and beat me, and thank and praise God if only I might live. My life is so unlived; I have never done anything for anybody, and now this useless life is going to end. If you knew how reluctant I am to die, maybe you would do something, do everything in your power. I don't suppose you can do anything, but I thought that if you and everyone else prayed for me and refused to let me go, then God would let me live. Oh, how grateful I would be then; I would never again hurt anyone, only smile at whatever was allotted to me, if only I were allowed to live.

Mama is sitting here weeping. She also sat here all last night and wept for me. This does me some good, it softens the bitterness of my passing. Today I thought: how would you like it if I came right up to you in the street one day when I was nicely dressed and no longer said anything hurtful but gave you a rose I had bought beforehand? But then the next moment I thought that I can never do what I want anymore, for I suspect I'll never get well again before I die. I cry so much, I lie still and cry without letup, inconsolably; it doesn't hurt my chest as long as I don't sob. Johannes, my dear, dear friend, my only beloved on earth, come to me now and stay with me for a moment when it begins to grow dark. I won't cry then, but smile as well as I can, for sheer joy at your coming.

Oh, where is my pride and my courage! I'm not being my father's daughter anymore; but that's because my strength is gone. I have suffered for a long time, Johannes, starting long before these last few days. I suffered when you were abroad, and later, since coming to the city in the spring, I have done nothing but suffer every day. I never knew before how infinitely long a night could be. I've seen you twice in the street during this time; once you were humming as you passed me, but you didn't see me. I was hoping to see you at the Seiers', but you didn't come. I wouldn't have spoken to you or come up to you, but been grateful just to see you at a distance. But you didn't come. Then I thought that perhaps it was because of me that you didn't come. At eleven o'clock I began to dance, because I couldn't bear to wait any longer. Yes, Johannes, I have loved you, loved only you all my life. It is Victoria who is writing this, and God is reading it over my shoulder.

And now I must say good-bye to you; it has grown almost dark and I cannot see any longer. Good-bye, Johannes, and thank you for every day. When I fly away from the earth, I'll go on thanking you till the very end and saying your name to myself all the way. May you find happiness in life, and forgive me for the wrong I've done you and for not having thrown myself at your feet and asked your forgiveness. I'm doing so now, in my heart. Live happily, Johannes, and good-bye for ever. And thank you once again for every single day and hour. I cannot go on.

Yours,
VICTORIA

Now the lamp has been lighted and things look much brighter. I've been lying in a trance and again been far away from the earth. Thank God, it wasn't quite as dreadful this time, I even heard some music, and above all it wasn't dark. I'm so grateful. But now I have no more strength left to write. Good-bye, my love. . . .